I0779399

LANA LYNNE

Moonlight and Freedom
By
Lana Lynne

Dedicated to

The men of the Third Arkansas Infantry Regiment
with a special affection for Company F from Rockport,
Arkansas and
The men of the Texas Brigade

Also,
My great-grandfather who served in Company C of the
Fourth Arkansas Infantry, as well as in Company B,
Witherspoon's Battalion, Arkansas Cavalry

Author's Acknowledgments and Notes

Moonlight and Freedom is the prequel to my first book and the other books in the five-book series. Each book can stand alone, but the characters were introduced in the first one. Numerous people have shared in the journey of this series, as well as in the development of my other novels and novellas.

For this book, I must go back to the beginning and thank my late Aunt Azalee Duke for her encouragement and help with research for the first book, *Home Always Beckons* (2009), (A second edition followed in 2018), as well as Brenda Matthews of the Malvern Chamber of Commerce who completed research for me and first introduced me to wonderful historical sources including numerous volumes of *The Heritage* published yearly by the Hot Spring County, Arkansas Historical Society in Malvern, Arkansas, as well as the *Malvern Daily Record, 50th, 1916-1966, Fiftieth Anniversary Edition, Volume Fifty-One, Number One*. During the research for this current novel, I found these resources helpful and delved deeper into other research more specific to the Civil War years in Arkansas. After searching for the availability of hard copies this year, I delighted in procuring a vintage copy of the *Malvern Daily Record, 50th, 1916-1966, Fiftieth Anniversary Edition, Volume Fifty-One, Number One* on sale online from a lady in Mt. Ida.

A timely email correspondence with Paul Adcox, Corresponding Secretary of the Hot Spring County, Arkansas Historical Society, and then an in-person meeting with Kinney Black, President of the Hot Spring County, Arkansas Historical Society this year allowed me to obtain hard copies of *The Heritage* volumes in which Brenda Matthews had originally found some of the background information for my first novel in 2009. I also discovered other helpful information and volumes with historical background applicable to the Civil War years in Arkansas. Some focused on Rockport, Arkansas, the setting for my home-front chapters and characters. I've listed the most helpful volumes of *The Heritage* discovered during my research under "Periodicals" in the Selected Bibliography and Further Reading section. Please visit the HSC Historical Society website to learn more about them: https://hschistoricalsociety.tripod.com/.

I am grateful for the confirmation and insight these volumes provided. They are listed in the Selected Bibliography for Further Reading section at the end of the book, along with other historical sources. Thank you to Aunt Azalee, Brenda Matthews, Paul Adcox, and Kinney Black.

Among the other listings, I must specify others assisting me in locating needed volumes for historical accuracy: Thank you to Pete Adams of Gladewater Books in Gladewater, Texas, for his help in locating a helpful, vintage research book; A heartfelt thank you to the Longview Public Library in Longview, Texas, for helping me find volumes of helpful research books and for procuring one on interlibrary loan; and Alan Thomson, my brother-in-law's brother, who shares my love of history and provided hard-to-find reprints of *Harper's Weekly,* as well as a rare book from 1899, *Official and Illustrated War Record* (this is the first part of the long title. See the Selected Bibliography Section for Further Reading for the complete title and information). *Note this is a large and very old book made available for my usage by Alan Thomson from his collection of books. I am thankful for the books and early magazines/newspaper reissues he also provided to me. This book is stamped with the following statement: "This work is sold by subscription only, and will never be for sale in book stores." It is in very poor condition with torn pages, unattached binding, mildew on edges, and a worn cover; however, the sketches are intact and beautiful—except for torn pages on the longer, foldable sketches. With the exception of the first few pages, all printed pages are legible and present. It is a rare opportunity to view and read the information and sketches therein.

I also wish to thank my sister and her husband for providing ongoing access to these.

One of the classic stories mentioned by one of my characters within this story is *Oliver Twist* by Charles Dickens. As some of my readers know, I am a huge fan of Dickens and have had my characters mention reading his stories in other books. The Selected Bibliography and Further Reading section at the back of the book lists the edition of the book I own. It is the edition released by Bantam Classic Edition in 1981 using the text from the 1867 publication. However, the reader may not be aware of the history of the publication of this classic story. Bantam lists a summary of the history of the progression of the printings starting first in 1837 to 1839 as "Oliver Twist; or, The Parish Boy's Progress" by Boz (a pseudonym for Charles Dickens) in the magazine *Bentley's Miscellany* with George

Cruikshank listed as the illustrator. It released as a three-volume novel in 1838 under the same title. In 1839, the second edition shortened the title to *Oliver Twist* and listed Charles Dickens without the use of a pseudonym. I looked up further history of the editions released and if interested, I encourage the reader to do so to learn more.

Some of his stories also ran in *Harper's Weekly*. I mention *Great Expectations*. Please see the *Harper's Weekly* information listed in the Selected Bibliography and Further Reading section to pursue more information. I've listed the issues containing his chapter installments through May 25, 1861, however, the chapters continued until August.

The diligent and astute critiques of my critique group always prove invaluable to me. I wish to thank Linda Burklin, Vickie Phelps, and Danyce Gustafson. Your knowledge and friendship refine my work. My gratitude is endless.

My editor, Sherri Stewart, is the sieve, sifting out the unnecessary, correcting the missed errors, and polishing the story. Her experience and intelligence refresh my eyes and heart each time I work with her.

My publisher, Cynthia Hickey, of Winged Publications, Forget-Me-Not-Romances imprint, is the captain at the helm of a ship holding a cargo of the treasured books of their authors—none of which make land and find their way into the hands of readers without her. Thank you for keeping me aboard and sailing on this journey with the Winged Publications family.

I wish to thank my father. It is by God's grace you and I are still here. You have inspired and encouraged me every step of the way.

I wish to thank my husband, Rick, for his patience, love, and willingness to read through my chapters. Your prayers and steadfastness have helped carry me through this year. You have protected, provided for, and cared for me during a year unlike any of the others we've shared. God blessed me to have you at my side.

At the beginning of the year, I didn't know if I'd finish this book. I'd started it a few years ago at the request of readers who wanted a prequel to the first book. They wanted to see the characters during the Civil War years.

This year has been "the year of the heart" for my family. I had open-heart surgery to replace a failing heart valve in May. The goodness of the Lord is beyond any words. He has carried me. I am humbled and grateful.

Delving into the lives of many of the real men, families, and communities who lived during the Civil War, and in particular the ones from Arkansas and Texas, connected me to them in visceral and unexpected ways. I found many wonderful books and sources, but if I had to name the books giving me the most intimate insight into the Third Arkansas Infantry and the Texas Brigade, the following led the way: *They'll Do To Tie To! Hood's Arkansas Toothpicks, Third Arkansas Infantry Regiment-C. S. A.* by Captain Calvin L. Collier, U.S. Air Force and *Hood's Texas Brigade: Its Marches, Its Battles, Its Achievements* by J.B. Polley. I've included a few of this group's well-known antics, but as my characters held more of the focus, these are limited. Please read these two books. You'll come away with a profound appreciation of the real men and a few laughs and tears.

The characters and background history of the Reconstruction-period books I'd written before had sparked an interest, admiration, and love of this period and the real people who lived during those years. However, my readers proved correct. Walking with my characters during the actual war years impacted me to a deeper level.

In trying to honor the real men who served in the Third Arkansas Infantry Regiment and those in the Texas Brigade, I strove to get the history and events correct. I hope I have succeeded, but this period is overwhelming in the details of each battle and their associated commanders, divisions, battalions, regiments, brigades, and companies. Any errors, omissions, or adjustments for the purpose of this fictional novel are my own.

The spellings of places or vocabulary usage differed at times, depending on the sources consulted. One example is the term 'litter-bearer' instead of 'stretcher-bearer' during this period. Even though the terms 'stretcher' and 'litter' are both found and used interchangeably, my research indicates the term 'litter-bearer' is the one used during the Civil War. Sometimes dates differed slightly. For example, the date the Third Arkansas became part of the Texas Brigade: Most have dated it in late November 1862, and one had an early December date in 1862 before the Battle of Fredericksburg commenced. I've gone with the majority consensus. In the case of Harper's Ferry vs. Harpers Ferry, I chose to go with the possessive form utilized until 1891 when the apostrophe was dropped. As my book is set in the 1860s, I wanted to use the form used at the time of the events. It is my hope that the Select Bibliography and Further Reading section at the end of the book will encourage you to read more of the actual history.

This is not a history textbook. It is a work of historical fiction with an endeavor to preserve and include some of the historical figures, places, and events as an authentic historical backdrop for my fictional characters' story. I haven't shown every engagement of the Third Arkansas Infantry Regiment but hope what I have included is sufficient to honor the real men, while focusing on the story of my characters.

I've made a list of my fictional characters to distinguish them from the multiple real historical commanders and figures associated with the military actions and armies of the Civil War. I started to provide a list of these commanders, but found even the ones I chose to use changed ranks so often it might overwhelm the reader. The real historical figures I've included within the story, each interacting with my characters, are by no means exhaustive and only represent some of the men involved in the history. Please go to the historic sources listed in the Selected Bibliography and Further Reading section to pursue more information.

One character included is half-and-half. Let me explain. Samuel H. Emerson was a real person who served in the Third Arkansas Infantry Regiment, Company F from Rockport, Arkansas. After he came home, he became the first mayor of Malvern once it was established. During the war, he suffered injuries, recovered, and continued to serve.

The character of "Sam" is a nod to him, but he is not the real person. I've shaped him and allowed him to interact with my characters a couple of times and to sustain like battle injuries. Since my fictional characters are supposed to be from Rockport, I wanted to honor Samuel H. Emerson and his life as so few of this distinguished regiment, and in particular the company from Rockport, made it home. I've read much about the Third Arkansas Infantry Regiment, including letters from members of Co. F, as well as its other companies. In my opinion, each person deserves to be remembered well.

My great-grandfather served in the Fourth Arkansas Infantry and Witherspoon's Battalion, Arkansas Cavalry as a Third Lieutenant. I've given a nod to him in the character of Arty (I must clarify that my great-grandfather's real name was Richard.) When I wrote my first book, the character of Richard was originally inspired by my great-grandfather, but their personalities are different—from what I know about him—and I placed the character of Richard in the Third Arkansas Infantry Regiment.

I have family who have lived in both of the counties these characters are from and hope I have honored them. We come from the legacies of our forefathers. None of us lived amidst the circumstances of the historic periods shaping their communities. We must look to the lives of the people of the period, learning from them—from both their regrets and their triumphs. Only God knows their hearts. Only God knows ours.

God Bless,

Lana Lynne

List of Fictional Characters:

Richard Cushman (He progresses from Private to Corporal to Sergeant.)
Alan Cushman (He progresses to the rank of Fourth Corporal.)
Ella Cushman
Dawn Cushman
Florence "Florey" Cushman
Alice Cushman

Jenny
Jenny's father/pa (He progresses to Sergeant.)

Alan Johnson
Emily Johnson
Marcus "Marc" Johnson (He progresses to Third Lieutenant.)
Will Johnson
Jack Johnson

Ephraim Johnson (He is a fictional member of the Fourth Arkansas Infantry; a nephew of Alan and Emily; and a cousin of Marc, Will, and Jack.)
Dan Johnson (Ephraim's younger brother)
Matilda (Dan's intended)

Carl Wilkins (He progresses to Fourth Corporal.)
Mary Wilkins
John Wilkins
Matt Wilkins

Private Bevil Henry (He progresses to the rank of Corporal.) (He is a fictitious member of the First Texas Infantry.)

Boyd Richards (Captain)
Nancy Richards (Boyd's wife, mentioned but never seen)
Sam Richards (Boyd and Nancy's son, mentioned but never seen)
Aunt Elizabeth Richards
Boyd's uncle (He isn't mentioned by name.)
Martha and Daniel (former slaves from Boyd's uncle's plantation)

Mrs. Bailey/Vera Bailey (postmistress)
Mrs. O' Neal (local store owner in Rockport)

Arnold Beasley

Arty (This character is inspired by my great-grandfather—his first name differed—who served in the Fourth Arkansas Infantry and later as a Third Lieutenant in Witherspoon's Battalion.)

*"Sam" (He is inspired by one of the real members of the Third Arkansas Infantry, Co. F, Samuel H. Emerson, but interactions and story actions with my characters are fiction. I do give a nod to his documented injuries sustained at Gettysburg and the Wilderness shown in Goodspeed's book—see Selected Bibliography and Further Reading section.)

Other peripheral characters:

Private Frank Duncan (Texan/Member of the
Texas Brigade)
Joe (Texan/Member of the Texas Brigade)

Chapter One

"Look at it, John. We sure ain't on the Arkansas anymore."

Richard Cushman grinned as Matt Wilkins ran from one side of the steamer ship to the other. He shook his burnished head at the exuberance of youth. He ambled over to where the boy's older brother stood. John Wilkins leaned against the rail next to his best friend, Marc.

The size of the Mississippi River awed all of them. The Ouachita back home had always seemed large and intimidating in the power of its current over the rocks at Rockport. Richard relished the memory of his boyhood fishing days, then glanced across the deck at his pa and Mr. Wilkins. They seemed oblivious to the youthful excitement, remaining engaged in deep conversation. Richard turned, jostling John Wilkins with his elbow before joining the group gathered at the rail.

"Your little brother's liable to fall overboard if he don't slow down."

His two boyhood friends turned to grin at him before their eyes cut to the thirteen-year-old reveling in discovery. Of course, being a few years older, none of them dared to admit the degree of excitement this new adventure stirred in the group—now known as Company F of the Third Arkansas Infantry.

Matt ran back to them, pushing between them to lean over the rail. "Florey would love this."

Richard resisted the impulse to ruffle the boy's hair. Instead, he met his twinkling brown eyes and nodded. "Yes, she would. I'm glad we managed to get on the boat without my little sister trying to follow us. If you see any delicate-looking soldiers, be sure it's not her in disguise."

Matt's eyes widened. "You don't think she'd do that, do ya? Aw, you're just funning."

Knowing his little sister, who shared his gray eyes and red-haired temperament, the distinct possibility did exist, but Richard found it doubtful. She looked younger than her twelve years to many because of her slight stature. As a result, many underestimated her. He never would. Florey had gumption.

A loud laugh from his tall friend Marcus, or Marc as he was known, caused them to turn. Others scurried across the deck to the other side of the boat at the sound of a splash.

His friend reached across him to give Matt a playful punch in the arm. "You'd better watch yourself—don't lean over too far."

Pools of laughter filled the deck.

The atmosphere of discovery and excitement lasted all the way to Memphis, Tennessee. There they left the steamer and boarded a train. Some rode in stock cars and others in passenger cars. However, following their arrival in Lynchburg, Virginia, on the third day of July, a slight apprehension began trickling through the men and boys from Rockport. None of them knew what to expect.

After a couple of weeks of intensive training, General William W. Loring became their new commander. The orders came for them to move out toward the mountains, and they boarded a train. The beautiful trip across a verdant countryside reminded Richard of the lush fields of Arkansas, but once they arrived, the challenges of the higher terrain, nonstop rain, and deep mud in the camp sobered him to their new reality.

Young Matt and a few others got sick. Sniffles turned into pneumonia, measles, or the pox. They lost two friends. Thankfully, and in no small part due to his older brother's prayers and care, Matt recovered.

Richard pretended not to notice when John hid half his rations in his haversack and ducked out of the tent at night to tend Matt.

The distant artillery and reports of battles signaled them to get ready. Their boasts lessened, even as their grips tightened on the long knives they brought from home. Rumors of their skills with the knives, as well as their accurate shooting skills from years of hunting back home, soon circulated. Richard shrugged at the praise. They'd all known how to use guns and knives almost from the day they'd learned to walk.

His friend Marc made the most of the attention, showing his superb skills, outshining everyone in the company. All who grew up in Rockport knew Marc couldn't help himself. No braggart intentions existed. Most of the others squelched the resentment they held as children when the oldest Johnson boy excelled at everything he tried because—Richard grinned thinking about it—Marc Johnson helped everyone, looked down on no one, and kept complaints to a minimum or turned them into a joke. Like this morning.

The rumbles of news or change trickled through the camp faster than the official announcements. Pigments of night still dotted the early dawn sky as they cleaned their mess kits after a sparse breakfast.

Marc inclined his head as John whispered the spreading news and then elbowed Richard. "Another change in staff. How can we even remember those leading thus far? Rust, Barton, Manning, Newman . . . Loring—and they keep changing rank. Who will be next? Maybe Jeff Davis himself will come here."

"I know." This time Richard gave his joking friend a smug smile. He'd overheard it from General Loring. Well, not from his actual lips, but from the camp doctor who'd heard it from the general. The expectant faces of his friends only allowed him to relish his knowledge for a moment before he said, "A new man will direct things. His name is Robert E. Lee. His sights are set on Cheat Mountain. I don't know if we'll see him, but our feet will respond to his orders and any man he sends to lead us." His friends' open mouths brought him some satisfaction.

"Never heard of him," Marc said.

Matt grinned. "I have. Heard he likes horses."

A familiar light shone in Marc's eyes. "Sounds like a good man."

"Yep—you've got something in common."

John bumped into his brother. "Don't encourage him."

Richard half hoped for the brothers' normal scuffling but knew friendly brawls were behind them for a time. The commanders had drilled any early unruly behavior out of them during training. He hoped any new generals they might have in the future allowed for a time to let off steam.

He might be able to ask his father. His pa and Mr. Wilkins had kept their distance ever since they left Rockport. They treated them like adults now. Since they were older, both men had received promotions to the rank of fourth corporal when sickness claimed more lives. The enemy of illness created needs in their ranks even before the battles did.

By August, Richard tired of their stay at Camp Bartow. It was pretty by the Greenbrier River, but sickness continued to overtake many of his friends. He also detested all the rain.

Another change in command tried his patience. General Loring placed them in Brigadier General Henry R. Jackson's Brigade, who, in turn placed them in a flanking position under Colonel Rust. A series of reality-inducing skirmishes, starting with the one at Cheat Mountain in September, soon seasoned him and his fellow farm boys.

They followed the plan of General Lee—never seeing him. After they endured a slippery climb up the mountain in cold rain and deep mud, adrenaline and panic fueled their advance toward the fighting as they descended the ledge.

Richard had never breathed so hard in his life. He marveled at their leader taking prisoners without all-out battle. Richard wiped the mud off his top lip as they waited for the colonel to question one of his talkative Yankee prisoners. He held his breath and remained quiet as ordered from their concealed positions in the bushes.

Marc elbowed him and whispered in his ear. "What's taking so long? Are we fighting or not?"

Richard shrugged and put his lips next to his friend's ear. "It don't make sense—we're leaving. Those Yanks don't know we're here. These heights have made our leader a bit squirrelly."

They shook their heads, not knowing whether to be relieved or mad when the retreat order came. Hours later they cursed under their breaths as they half fell down the mountain, toppling over each other in the pitch-black night. Apprehension churned Richard's insides on the long way back to camp.

A month later, along the roads and in the forests of their prior, abysmal battle failure, they crested the Greenbrier riverbank as the enemy's artillery sent them into the closest ditch. They lay on their bellies, muskets prepared. After the Yankees started crossing the river, their colonel positioned them for battle. Soon, the reality of other boys and men trying to kill them steadied their guns as they fired as one. Beside him, Matt lowered his gun for a moment after the first round of firing.

"They fell. We killed 'em—I—" The youth's round brown eyes stared without blinking.

Richard glanced at the fallen men, but kept reloading. "Matt, reload."

John grabbed his brother's gun, reloaded it, and shoved it back just as the command to fire came.

The volley of gunfire and exploding cannon shells made Richard's ears ring, the stench of gunpowder stinging his nose. His chest heaved in the cold October air following the enemy's retreat, even as he reloaded again. Then he forgot to breathe as he kept reloading and taking cover for the next couple of hours under the Federal retaliation. His peripheral vision assured him his best friends remained in motion as they battled beside him.

They heard the retreat sound for the boys in blue. Boys—no. Richard could no longer think of the men he faced that way. The enemy label fit them. Forget about being proper with titles such as Federals or Union troops. He spat on the ground. "Just Yankees."

"Where?" Marc gripped the barrel of his gun next to him and peeked over the dirt bank.

Richard hadn't realized he'd spoken the words aloud. He elbowed Marc, shaking his head. "No, they're retreating. We showed them Yankees."

Marc grinned back at him. John gave him a brief, cautious smile and then scanned the river and trees before slapping his brother on the shoulder. Matt rolled over on his side, peering down their ranks. His face remained pale, even with a nose reddened from the cold, then he inclined his head. "We lost some."

In the absence of close artillery sounds, a few moans reached Richard's ears for the first time. "Naw, they're just wounded. If any of our troops fell, it'd have to be the Georgians or Virginians. Arkansans are too tough to die."

Matt gave him a half grin that faded as he looked at the blue uniformed boy lying just in front of him. Richard watched in disbelief as Matt leaned forward and lifted the flap on the fallen soldier's haversack. No one spoke as the youth took out a piece of paper, read it, and then returned it. John met Richard's eyes as Matt sat back, pulling his knees up. They waited.

Matt peered up, tears streaming down his face. "Indiana. He was from Indiana. His mother told him to be careful."

Before anyone could respond, Marc jumped up from beside Richard and jerked Matt to his feet. The sound of the slap stunned those within range.

"You stop it this instant, Matt Wilkins. We promised your ma we'd bring you home. That won't happen if you think about the mothers of every enemy soldier you kill." He jerked Matt over to the fallen soldier and pulled him down, inches from the boy's open but lifeless blue eyes. "This boy would have killed you. I don't know if you shot him or if I did. All I know is I want all of the Confederate boys to go home to their mothers. You can't think about anything else. In the Bible, when King David took his men to battle, he didn't check on his enemies as they fell. You'll get us all killed, Matt, if you do."

The colonel approached but Richard couldn't find his voice in time, and the officer heard all of Marc's last words to Matt.

"Soldier, is there a problem?"

Marc dropped Matt's arm, as they all came to attention. "No, sir."

Colonel Barton gave a curt nod. "Good. All of you men are to be commended today." Once the colonel turned, his lieutenant gave the order to fall into ranks.

That night in camp, Richard lay reading the small Bible John's ma had sent with them to share. He looked up as a figure blocked the lantern. "Hey." Richard swallowed his words as his pa, Alan Cushman, sat down on his blanket. He sat up, closing the sacred book, then met his pa's concerned gaze.

"How are you faring, son?"

"Honestly, sir?"

"Of course."

"Wondering if my heart isn't as tender as it should be."

"Why's that?"

Richard scratched his head, adjusting so he could face his father. "Well, I'm eighteen-years-old and have never killed anything but varmints. Killing a man should have given me pause today. It didn't. I stopped thinking and just reacted. Anyway, it's not just me. Marc took to it like some contest he had to win. What's wrong with us?"

His pa glanced at the Bible. "What were you reading?"

Guilt nearly choked him. "I guess I was searching the battles in the Good Book to vindicate my feelings."

An understanding smile flashed on his father's face. "Did it?"

Richard released his breath. "That's the bad part. It kinda did in one way. The battles directed with God's guidance did. It's just, in reading this, it's clear who fought on God's side. I don't know how we can decide who is pleasing God in all of this—the Yankees or us?"

"You can't, son. Neither can I. But I do know we are to be subject to those who rule us."

"What if you disagree?"

"Do you, Richard? I've always loved our country, but now that country has divided. After I studied the agendas of both governments, I considered my community and family's needs. We've never owned slaves, son, and never will. That's not my fight. My fight is in the right to build the economy within the Southern states in the way each of those individual states finds best for their citizens. That means if they decide one crop is better than multiple crops, it should be up to them. The point is the individual states should decide. The only problem I can see with each states' vehement hold on their individual rights—as far as winning this war is concerned—is this: Will they give President Davis the national right he needs to run the South?"

"I agree, Pa. Still, why didn't I want to cry like Matt? Who knows how John feels? He keeps quiet about everything."

His pa chuckled as Marc and John entered, followed by Matt and his father, Carl Wilkins. "Oh, he does? Marc's bloody nose speaks loud enough."

Richard saw a cut on John's lip and grinned. They all had a history of settling things with their fists, but it always took a lot to rile John. Unlike Marc and him, who took to fighting like birds to flight. Realization registered. He laughed, and Marc glared at him.

"No, no, it's not about you, Marc. Well, maybe a bit."

Marc wiped his nose with his bandana and plopped down on his wool blanket.

Matt smiled at Richard before sitting down beside Marc. "Thanks for trying to help, Marc. Sorry about your nose."

Marc shrugged. "Just trying to keep you alive, kid. But—"

"Next time, you'll let *me* tend to my brother," John finished for Marc.

Richard handed the Bible to Matt. "This might help."

Carl Wilkins nodded to his boys and Marc before joining Mr. Cushman by the tent flap. Carl didn't say anything. They sure were a quiet family who settled things in a different manner than his.

Richard shook his head and smirked. His friends laughed. "Move over, Marc, you're on my blanket." He blew out the lantern and snickered when Marc elbowed him.

By the end of the next six or seven weeks, he stopped laughing when a few men from the multiple companies of the Third Arkansas died each week. The enemy of sickness had once again invaded the troops staying in the region of the Alleghenies. His insides crawled with the turmoil of grief and the claustrophobic suffocation of camp life.

Writing letters home kept him from pacing like a trapped mountain lion. If he kept his heart set on where he wanted to be and the future he planned, it calmed him. Richard wrote his ma and sisters every day, as well as a series of daily letters he never planned to mail. He'd just finished one of these inconsequential letters and sat pondering the possible reaction of the young lady. Guilt and embarrassment coursed through him when he saw his pa squatting down by the fire in front of him. He shoved the letter in his haversack and stood.

"Sit down, Richard." Pa finished pouring his cup of treasured coffee, squinted, and blew on the steaming liquid for a minute. "Do you want me to mail that letter?" He took a sip. "I can tell her pa I approved it."

Richard's mouth went dry. "No, sir."

His father shrugged. "Fine. You let me know if you change your mind." He turned to go and then turned back. "Oh, I almost forgot. I received a letter from Jenny's pa today. He hopes to join us soon. It looks like Mr. Johnson is recovering well from his illness, and they might be able to take care of young Jenny for him."

No, that wasn't a good idea. Those younger brothers of Marc's would bother her to no end. "She won't like that, Pa."

His pa's eyebrow lifted. "Why?"

"Well . . . she just won't."

"Maybe, you should write and ask her."

Richard glanced at his haversack. "No, she's not expecting to hear from me."

His father nodded. "Suppose you know best. I guess it won't matter—"

A lump rose in his throat. "What won't matter, Pa?"

"Jenny asked him to send her regards to you."

His heart thudded. "She did?"

"Yes, son. Now, get ready. We're marching out today."

Chapter Two

Mud oozed between Jenny's toes. She ran along the muddy path toward her abandoned house, searching for the younger girl, now obscured by the torrential rain.

"Florey, be careful. Your ma will have our hides."

The dark shape of the cabin loomed in contrast to the sheets of rain. She reached the porch, pushing her soaked hair away from her face. The rain had destroyed the more refined coil she'd recently adapted in lieu of her usual single braid.

"You're a mess."

She glanced up at the younger girl leaning against the door. The thirteen-year-old facing her wore a satisfied grin, visible in the shadow of the floppy, brimmed hat covering her amber hair.

Jenny reached over and removed the hat. "And you look like a boy dressed like that."

One copper braid tumbled out, cascading down the girl's back. A mock glare and quick swipe by the shorter girl made Jenny laugh. "Richard won't like his little sister wearing his clothes."

"He's fighting the Yankees his way, and I'm fighting them my way. I ain't staying home because they're roaming around." Florey swiped her forehead with the back of her hand. "I'm glad you feel the same."

Jenny bit her lip. "Well, I wouldn't say that exactly. It's just those persistent Johnson brothers have made it their mission to look out for me this past year. Even after my pa waited to join up until yours came home. Tell me again about how your pa got injured."

Her younger friend sighed. "I get confused about much of the war stuff. He won't talk about it in front of us, but I overheard him talking to your pa before he left. They went through a tough winter campaign under Stonewall Jackson. It was so bad. They marched in extreme ice and cold. Marc Johnson almost got in trouble because of speaking out about the cruelty the horses endured in those conditions. Leave it to Marc. He loves horses.

"Anyway, they've been a part of so many brigades, it makes my head hurt to think about it. But they finally left the cold valley and mountain conditions after winter. Do you remember when some of the men came home for a bit? Pa winked and said *that* furlough offer somehow didn't impact the Cushmans, Wilkins, or Johnsons. Let's see—"

Jenny rolled her eyes. "Florey, just tell me about how he got injured."

Her friend's concentration-induced frown disappeared after another moment. "Oh yeah, they sent more money home about that time. Anyway, they marched under this commander and then many different ones. Major Manning did a good job.

"Pa was injured during that terrible winter campaign when they were with General Jackson and Colonel Rust. There was something about a bridge, a river, and a skirmish. That's where he was injured in the knee. Just about destroyed it. Some other men also got shot." Gray eyes looked straight at her. "Did you know Richard got shot in the arm there, but it missed the bone and went straight through?"

Jenny's mouth went dry, and she fought for enough saliva to swallow. "No, no one told me. Is he recovered?"

Florey walked over and took her hand. "Yes, but I don't want to talk about this anymore. My brother, your pa, and the others will all come back fine. Your father didn't want you to worry when he left. He knew Pa would take care of you."

Jenny smiled. "You're right. How's Matt?"

Florey smiled. "Just fine. Pa says he's a wonderful soldier."

She didn't want to pry, but her friend wasn't saying something. "Has he written to anyone lately?"

"Well, they've been very busy. He's doing a man's job. Has Richard written you?"

Her heart twisted. "No, that wouldn't be proper. Nevertheless, he does send his regards in the letters from my father. That's why I wanted to come up here today. Pa told me all the letters he'd received from your pa and the few friends he has are stored in our trunk.

Plus, those old copies of *Harper's Weekly* Mrs. Bailey loaned me.

"She isn't sure if she'll continue her subscription after this year, given the pointed editorial addressing Southern subscribers and the magazine declaring their loyalty to the Union in May. Mrs. Bailey knows I love reading, and they have featured chapters from the book *Great Expectations* by Mr. Charles Dickens, the English writer, in their publication each month. We don't want any Yankees getting them now that no one is living here." She pushed open the cabin door. "You wait here. Holler if anyone comes. I'll hurry."

She didn't wait for Florey to answer. Regardless of her friend's bravado, the tension of the unknown surrounded them. One never knew who was behind the next tree. Thankful she knew every inch of the cabin in the dark as well as the light, she wouldn't light a lantern.

The trunk sat under the uncovered window near the washstand. Even with the storm-darkened sky, dim illumination streaked through the windowpane enough to aid her in her task. Jenny fumbled with the latch and raised the heavy lid. She grabbed the cloth sack holding the letters from the bottom and lowered the lid.

"Jenny!" Florey hissed, leaning in the door just as she turned. "Somebody's coming."

She hurried to the door, shut it behind her, and grabbed Florey by the hand. They dashed off the porch and then slithered under it. If those Yankees had ears, they'd be sure to hear them breathing and their hearts beating.

The two horses bearing boys in blue passed the cabin. The soldiers hunched close over their mounts against the deluge of rain.

Jenny and Florey waited, clinging to each other. Of course, the thudding only resonated within, and Jenny exhaled once the horses disappeared. "Let's go the back way," she whispered.

Florey nodded, eyes wide, and stayed behind her until they ducked out from under the porch, but then Florey dashed ahead. *That headstrong girl!*

Jenny raced to catch up to her on the downward path behind the cabin.

Chapter Three

The incessant desire to scratch the vermin plaguing him almost got him shot. Richard suppressed his fingers; instead, he used his sharpshooter skills on Gill's Bluff. Marc fired his weapon beside him. The Yank heads appearing from the gunboats looked like moles popping out of their holes. Squirrels, moles, and men were all the same to the Rockport boys. Screams came from the boat and shore. Matt whooped when a white flag appeared but reloaded when the boat started to move. John stood when the useless boat floated to the side.

Richard wiped his nose with the back of his hand and scrambled to his feet. "That'll show 'em." A bittersweet satisfaction filled him.

The months leading to this day had been educational but grievous—marching and drilling in Colonel Taliaferro's Brigade in November and then starving and freezing with Stonewall Jackson during the harsh winter months. Marc had come near to getting into trouble when the freezing horses were pushed beyond consideration.

In January, they'd started the year in the frigid cold with a skirmish near Bath. The day after the battle rankled Richard. Jackson ordered Colonel Rust to lead them in a late afternoon and evening maneuver to destroy a railroad bridge over the Cacapon River. Canister shot injured two from other companies in the Third Arkansas, and Federal snipers shot his father in the knee and him in the arm. Pa's injury sent him home, but Richard's arm healed quick, the bullet merely grazing the upper part.

By the first week of January, Richard almost failed to hold his temper in check. They'd nearly froze them on the picket lines due to a decree forbidding fires one night. The next day they'd marched to Romney, and that's when Marc had a fit about the animals' treatment.

Praise the Lord for the efforts of Colonel Rust, General Loring, and Major Manning on their behalf. The Third Arkansas didn't have to remain there.

After departing from the arduous company of Jackson in February, they moved under the division command of General T. H. Holmes. They went by train to a camp outside of Fredericksburg. None of them could believe their luck in finding fellow Arkansas boys in the camp—The First Arkansas Regiment. Richard smiled every time he thought about their visit with them.

In March, more changes came, including the promotion of Major Manning to Colonel, who took over their regiment. Richard liked and admired him.

Richard just whistled and smiled when some of his fellow soldiers grumbled when other changes within the companies occurred, albeit by resignation or promotion. Complaining never changed anything in the military.

Between then and today's fine shooting, they'd followed orders, burning trains and supplies to keep them from reaching the enemy. Relief came when their next train ride took them to a warmer camp—Goldsboro. Richard wrote letters about their new brigade commander, General J. G. Walker, and adjusted to more changes.

Matt laughed and asked, "Whose brigade are we in this week?"

In late May, they had boarded a train, bringing them back to Virginia. They'd itched for action but were put on work detail setting up artillery and infantry positions at Drewry's Bluff instead. The Army commander, General Joseph E. Johnston directed all actions, which they followed, shovels in hand. The Third Arkansas dug while the Second Arkansas Battalion fired many a shot.

Bloody and deadly action ensued. The Second Arkansas Battalion took part, but Richard's company didn't. They could hear the explosions and yells of the battle. General Johnston fell at Fair Oaks-Seven Pines with severe wounds. Robert E. Lee replaced him. Richard had hoped to meet him this time, but instead settled for following his orders—to keep digging trenches.

By June, Richard had just about tired of the shovels. John never said much, but even he agreed. The Federal gunboats had caused problems, and their command needed fortified positions on both Drewry and Gill's Bluffs. This had led to today.

Richard spat on the ground thinking of the Yankee, General McClellan. Marc nudged him with his elbow. "Quit thinking so much. Enjoy this!"

Richard laughed.

Marc blinked and joined him, as did Matt and John. The too rare sound of laughter trickled throughout the Hot Spring Hornets' company ranks.

Another friend fell in step beside Richard. "This was more fun than that card game in March. They stopped our knife fight, but no one stopped us today." Richard shouldered his gun.

Marc pulled out his knife. "*This* so-called Arkansas Toothpick is overdue for some action."

Around them, heads nodded.

Richard took a breath. "Better put that away. Let the battles find us."

Marc's eyes met his, but he complied. "They will."

Matt swiped the hair off his forehead. "Wonder where we're heading next?"

Silence overtook the group the rest of the way back to camp.

They soon found out when they moved from sharpshooting action to a few peaceful bivouac days, remaining near Drewry's Bluff. Richard enjoyed meeting boys from North Carolina, but he'd learned not to get too close. Men died. Friends perished. A tentative status of strangers with familiar faces worked better.

His mind registered the names of the additional commands—D. H. Hill, A. P. Hill, Longstreet, and grimaced when Stonewall Jackson's name continued to emerge. No denying his skills, but the memory of that terrible first winter campaign stayed with Richard.

The noise and activity in their bivouac increased. Horses rode in and out, their riders bringing news and orders. The Second Arkansas Battalion moved out to join General A. P. Hill's Light Division.

Plans for White Oak Swamp, Meadow Bridge, Beaver Dam, Mechanicsville, Turkey Creek, and Malvern Hill trickled through the camps.

The captain told them to stay ready to march. Long and even short marches to varied locales had long lost the initial excitement for the men when traveling to new places. All roads brought Richard and his friends in the Third to one destination—observation of battles, participation in skirmishes, and experiencing the aftermath of battle. The first rankled him. He'd rather fight.

A loud battle cry sounded in the distance— probably the Second Arkansas Battalion. He remembered the commanders looking at the maps and talking. They must be near Meadow Bridge at the Chickahominy River, or maybe they'd reached Beaver's Dam Creek.

Richard jumped when more artillery and gunfire sounded as he cooked a meager meal. The humid air carried the ever-present stench of battle and death. It hovered in his nostrils. Listening to battle unnerved him. He squeezed his fist.

Marc cleared his throat. "Don't worry; it's coming for us."

Richard stuffed a bite of barely cooked bacon and half a hard cracker in his mouth, then stuffed the rest of his rations in his haversack. He reached inside his bedroll for the letter he'd received. His correspondent came from a neighboring county and served in Company C of the Fourth Arkansas Infantry.

"Who's that from?" Marc squatted beside him.

"You remember Arty from near Montgomery County?"

Marc squinted. "Tall boy with hair redder than yours?"

Richard pushed his friend, laughing when he toppled. "Yeah." He glanced back at the page. "He's got dysentery bad. They might send him home."

Marc rolled on his side and propped up on one elbow. "That's rough. Might be lucky though."

"Nuh-huh." Richard shook his head. "You don't mean that. We've seen what it can do." He took another bite of the tasteless biscuit.

"Will he return or just stay home?"

Richard shrugged. "Can't say, but knowing him, he'll try to rejoin. Say a prayer for him."

Silence.

"Marc?" He folded the letter.

"I'm struggling with that a bit." Marc drew aimless circles in the dirt with a stick.

Richard scooted toward him and pulled him by his shirt front. "Do it anyway."

Marc jerked away. He shut his eyes, then disappeared into the darkness.

Richard took his own advice. Later that night, he lay on his blanket, staring at the star-filled sky. Gruesome memories of the dead bodies of some known and some unknown soldiers from other battalions haunted him. He had no desire to be among them, but he sure wanted more action than a shovel in his hands. Sharpshooting from the bluff had felt good.

"Hey, Richard."

He turned his head to the whispered entreaty. "Yeah, Matt?"

"I'm bothered."

"'Bout what?"

"I enjoyed the skirmish the other day. It's getting easy to kill other men."

Richard frowned in the darkness. "You can't say that. We've seen the results of it more than causing it. Talk to the Second Battalion. It seems they're seeing action every battle."

"I know. You think they're holding us in reserve?"

"They used us on Gill's Bluff."

"That's different. In fact, that's my point. I could serve as a sharpshooter for the rest of the war and not mind it."

Richard took a deep breath. *He's not wrong.* "How does John feel about it?"

A faint chuckle followed. Sounds of recognizable snores from the far side of Richard gave him the answer. Matt's hushed tones followed. "He's taking it in stride."

The unsettled stirrings within him calmed. A star twinkled, catching his gaze. Richard smiled. "I prayed earlier. Quit looking for trouble. Stop believing all your emotions. None of us ever prepared to be soldiers, but we are. Trust our commanders, but trust God more. He'll get both sides through it—some He'll gather to His home, and some get to go back to their towns and communities at the end. We don't get to decide which."

The heat of breath and Marc's voice came close to his ear. "You two had better be quiet. The way they're losing men, we'll all be in the thick of it soon enough."

Richard applied his elbow to the soft mid-section of his friend.

"Hmpf." Marc rolled away.

He grinned "G'night."

Matt chuckled. "Good night."

Richard's smile faded in the darkness, unsure of what the impending dawn march might bring. Would it bring fighting or a grim observation of the aftermath?

Chapter Four

Creak, jostle, creak. The wagon wheels protested against the muddy bog of the Arkansas road in the early dawn hours.

"I don't feel like—"

"Hush your mouth, boy. You stop your grumbling. I'm sure your brother and the rest of our boys don't feel like whatever they're facing today."

"Yes, Pa. Still, why—"

Thud. Jenny turned in time to see Will Johnson roll to his feet from his toppled position on the road. She knelt and touched Mr. Johnson's shoulder from her place in the back of the wagon. "You've lost one of your sons."

"Whoa!" Mr. Johnson pulled on the reins. He shifted around on the wagon seat. Beside him, Mr. Cushman did the same.

Seated on the back edge of the wagon, Jack Johnson laughed. "Pa told you to quit complaining. *I* taught you."

"Boy, you let me do the teaching."

Jack stopped laughing. "Yes, sir."

"Will, get back in this wagon. You boys will get us shot if you don't quit fooling around. We need to move that tree off the road and then head home."

Jenny stifled a yawn. She'd gotten up when Florey shook her shoulder in the wee hours. Trepidation of what lay ahead plagued her. They never knew if Federals or their dear boys-in-gray lurked in the trees or might meet them on the road.

One of the trees on Mr. Cushman's property had fallen during the storm yesterday evening. He said dawn was a better time to clear it than dusk. With his injured knee, he could no longer do things as quickly as he once did.

Mr. Johnson readily agreed to help when they went by early and roused his boys to come along. Jenny and Florey always helped these days. Dawn, Florey's older sister, as well as her youngest sister, Alice, remained home to work with their ma.

Florey giggled when Will scrambled back onto the wagon. Jack turned and grinned at them.

When Will punched Jack's arm, Mr. Johnson didn't even turn around. "Cut it out, boys. My back strap is under my seat."

Jenny shook her head and put her finger to her lips when Florey's eyes sparkled her way. She glanced ahead of them as the wagon slowed. A large black walnut tree blocked their path. A tingle of apprehension straightened her spine. Everyone else in the wagon straightened as well. She held her breath. The whack of an ax on the other side of the tree reverberated in the air.

Mr. Johnson shifted on his seat. "You children stay here until we find out who it is."

Mr. Cushman put a hand on his arm. "Better call out. Everyone's jumpy."

"Good morning!" Mr. Johnson jumped to the ground. "Can I help?"

The rhythmic sound of the ax stopped. "Who are you?"

"Lee Johnson."

The leaves on one of the downed branches shook, and a thatch of red hair pushed through followed by the face of a grinning young man. "Mr. Johnson. It's Arty."

Mr. Cushman eased himself to the ground and hobbled forward. "Your pa told me you came home real sick."

"Yeah, that was in June. I've rested a few months. Once the doctor says I'm strong enough, I'll head back. I hope to be in the cavalry this time."

"What are you doing working on this tree?"

"It blocked Pa and me yesterday. We were headed to the mill in Rockport, but we changed our minds when we found this." He grabbed a branch. "We whacked on it a bit then, but it got dark, so I came back this morning."

"Much appreciate it, but as it fell from my land, we'll take care of it."

Will and Jack scrambled out of the wagon. "Hey, you seen our brother?"

Jenny and Florey followed.

Arty dusted bits of tree bark off his shirt. "Naw, I was in the Fourth Infantry. I fought at Pea Ridge and a few other places. I sent Richard a letter before they sent me home. Haven't heard back though." He nodded at Will and Jack. "How old are you?"

Will grabbed his suspenders. "I'm twelve. 'Bout to be thirteen."

Arty winked. "If this war keeps going, you might get your chance to go." A haunted look appeared on his face, and he lowered his head.

Jenny's heart lurched.

Jack cleared his throat, his head an inch over his stockier brother. "I'm ten. Turn eleven soon enough."

Mr. Johnson shook his head. "Boys, grab the gear. We don't have time to visit."

Jack and Will peered back at Arty but headed to the wagon. Few made Mr. Johnson repeat his requests twice. He was a firm but fair man, and he loved his family. Jenny liked him almost as much as Mr. Cushman. Both men had been good friends to her pa.

Arty lifted his chin toward Mr. Cushman. "A minié ball shatter that knee?"

Mr. Cushman rubbed the knee in question. "Yep." He shut his eyes. "One minute you're running into the fray, and the next you're being pulled to safety—if you're lucky. Funny thing is our Rockport group had only seen mild action compared to the rest when I got hit, but it only takes a little action. One year of war was enough for me 'cause the knee and dysentery sent me home."

Arty nodded. "That last one's what got me, but I'm almost back to full strength. Ready to go again. Can't stay here with my friends all fighting."

Mr. Johnson rubbed the back of his neck and looked away. Jenny remembered how ill he, Will, and Jack had been at the time his oldest son Marc had marched off to war with the rest. He'd wanted to go, but the circumstances within the community pulled at him more than the need to go after he got well. It had to chafe him a bit.

"Pain is a funny thing, Arty." Mr. Cushman's eyes remained fixed on the young man. "Never thought I could hurt so bad, but once you experience it, your body starts bracing for it. It becomes almost normal. You know what I mean?"

The red-headed young man tilted his head. "Not like you do or the others I saw injured in battle. Hope I never get hit that way, but I know what it's like for your innards to be scalded and twisted 'til you can't even stand."

Jenny wiped the unheeded tears from her face.

Mr. Johnson cleared his throat. "Gentlemen, we have the girls with us."

Arty swallowed hard and backed toward the fallen tree. "Begging your pardon, girls." He climbed through the branches, and the methodical sound of an ax resumed.

Mr. Cushman joined Jenny in front of the wagon and placed a gentle hand on her shoulder. "You okay, sweet girl?"

She nodded. "It just made me think about what could be happening to Richard and my pa right now—the other boys too."

He patted her shoulder. "You just leave that in the good Lord's hands." His eyes darted to the smaller branches Arty had stacked to the right side of the road.

"You girls put those small branches in the back of the wagon. We might can split them for some kindling later."

Florey ran to the wagon and came back with a small hatchet. "I can do that now, Pa."

Mr. Cushman chuckled. "Let's just get the road cleared first. You can whack on those tonight if you want." He took the hatchet from her. "Now, get going on moving those branches."

Jenny smiled and prepared for the grumbling sure to follow. Florey loved to work right alongside the men. She remembered how her now thirteen-year-old friend had tagged along on most of the boys' fishing trips. Jenny would never have thought to be so bold.

Jenny had adored Richard ever since that day in the schoolyard when he'd rescued her—the new girl at school—from the bullies who didn't like half Indians like herself. She'd been only ten. He'd been fourteen—the same age she'd been when he marched away a little over a year ago. She'd never seen an eighteen-year-old as handsome as Richard.

Florey bumped her with her elbow. "Quit mooning over my brother. We've got work to do."

Jenny laughed. "I'm coming."

Chapter Five

Nightmares danced through Richard's slumber. The chill of the November night cooled his sweaty brow but did little to dissipate the memories of the past few months. The gruesome aftermath of the end of August's Battle of Second Manassas replayed. Flies on bodies strewn across the eerie silence of the battlefield, decimated munitions, and dead horses greeted their arrival in early September. He twisted his head from side to side in his sleep. The stench. Bile rose in his throat, waking him. He'd never forget that day.

They'd marched with gumption to join General Lee, emboldened with expanded numbers. Their ranks now included the remaining members of the brave men from the Second Arkansas Infantry Battalion who had lost their commander, Major Bronaugh, and many men during the Seven Days Battles. They'd joined them in July and helped complete the trench-digging to strengthen the defense of Richmond and Petersburg. Fine men all.

The camaraderie flowed with ease among them. Even those seasoned battlefield fighters had paled at the scene they found at Second Manassas. Matt had checked to see that there were no living among the fallen. Marc had checked the downed horses.

Their commanders had moved them onward toward Lee's intended invasion of Maryland. Grim determination burned in Richard's stomach. The troops sang songs of home and lost loves, reflecting on the men who'd never return. Richard's trigger finger itched to explode a charge into a bluebelly.

By the time they reached their destination, a group of grim, ill-clothed, and worn soldiers met them, but morale remained high. All eyes and ears fixed on General Lee's plans to capture Harper's Ferry. Captain Reedy led them across the Potomac. They'd marched with Walker's Brigade, led by their own beloved Colonel Manning.

Richard pinched the space between his eyes and reached under his blanket to rub his feet. He grinned. The rocky roads on his bare feet back on that September 12th day had toughened them ten-fold.

He chuckled at the memory of the events of the next day when they'd mistaken the stampede of a herd of livestock for the enemy cavalry. The rest of the troops had teased them about it and still did. It became an infamous joke sure to be retold after the war.

The next day, September 14th, the unmistakable sound of real battle had reached them. General Walker, General A. P. Hill, General Jackson, and more commanders directed every aspect of the battle. The list of master battle strategists made Richard's head spin. The multiple artillery batteries did the communicating and fighting. The commanders found no need to engage their Arkansas infantry. The Battle of Harper's Ferry ended the following day, and they hurried to Sharpsburg.

Marc stirred on his bedroll beside him and propped up on one elbow. "What's wrong?"

Richard shook his head. "Another nightmare."

"About the aftermath of Manassas or Sharpsburg?"

"Second Manassas and replaying everything since then." Richard pulled up his blanket against the chill of the late November breeze and met Marc's steady gaze. "Since we fought at Sharpsburg, you'd think I'd have nightmares about that, wouldn't ya?"

Marc gave a half-shrug. "In my opinion, we helped save the day at Sharpsburg by fighting alongside those North Carolina boys. They should have let us fight sooner. Our gray-lines had the toughest brigades, batteries, and division-fighting to win, but they were struggling when they sent us in. That changed things."

Richard strained in the dark, trying to visualize the bedrolls no longer present. "Yep, but it cost us."

Marc clenched his jaw. "War costs." His eyes flicked back toward Richard. "I sure admired Longstreet and Hood's men and Colonel Cook in the midst of it all."

Richard grinned. "Not the wobbly rider who came riding through?"

Marc smirked. "Hardly."

"I hated it when Colonel Manning got wounded."

"He's tough."

Matt stirred, and John tossed a stick at them. Richard reclined and pillowed his head on his arm. Marc rolled closer to him. "Are you ready to meet our new leaders and troops from Hood's Texas Brigade?"

Richard swallowed hard. "Doesn't matter. They change like bathwater." Realization dawned on him. "They fought at Second Manassas and Sharpsburg, didn't they?"

Silence hung between them for a moment. "Yeah."

Marc scooted back on his blanket.

Sleep came slow. Morning came fast.

They marched the miles toward the Texas Brigade's camp with a mixture of excitement and trepidation. Richard eyed the mostly smiling faces of the ranks turned out to meet them.

The Texans called out jokes and good-natured teasing, but one remark caught Richard's attention: "Here comes the Third Texas—they ain't Arkansas Toothpicks anymore." Although said in a friendly way, it rankled him a bit. They could label them whatever they wanted, but—

"He's got mountain-lion eyes." The whispered comment from Matt shifted his fixed gaze. The hatless blond-haired man's golden gaze remained steady. He spoke. "Gentlemen, fall in. Let's see some ranks." That wasn't a Texas accent, more like that from the vicinity of Georgia. Richard had met enough from the area in this war to recognize it.

Another officer stepped forward. "Men, this is Captain Boyd Richards of Hood's Texas Brigade. Although, technically non-commissioned, he has steadily moved up the ranks due to his exemplary behavior and skills, as well as the necessity created by the losses our fine men have suffered. His uncle owns one of the largest plantations in Georgia."

Richard observed the steel look of disgust from the captain before it flickered and died under a clenched, emotionless expression. Interesting. With the casualties and frequent combining of brigades, legions, and infantry, Richard had almost quit trying to remember all the new names and faces. But this man—he had a story. Richard loved solving a mystery.

Then the captain spoke. "We heard about those within your ranks. You'll do fine with our Texas Brigade." He grinned. "Your sharpshooting skills, your wicked knives, and—" He cocked an eyebrow. "Your rumored prowess of borrowing a few items or animals from surrounding farms."

Richard could sense the tension in the unusual quietness of the men surrounding him.

The Georgian-accented voice continued. "We won't mind some fresh bacon every now and again."

A collective exhale, including his own, released, followed by a few snickers. Richard cut his eyes toward Marc. His friend had refused to eat such provisions at first, but hunger pushed a man's conscience. Marc shook his head once and tipped the front of his recently acquired Third Lieutenant's hat downward.

Marc's skill with horses and ability to teach the green soldiers who joined their ranks had not gone unnoticed. Even though they were infantry, the officers had designated him to care for their horses and guide the newcomers. Mounts could make the difference in a battle. Marc's steady rise in the ranks had moved him from private status and had gleaned him the respect of their company, as he climbed the non-commissioned ladder throughout the months to reach his current esteemed status. Richard could tell today had spun his friend off-kilter. They were the newcomers this time.

The captain welcomed them and then introduced the available higher-ranked officers. Richard listened to their plans and where they'd be positioned — a central position—with Stonewall Jackson's Corps to their right and Longstreet's Corp—Pickett's Division to be exact—to their left.

Richard swallowed hard and directed a soft statement toward Matt. "No more digging trenches all day or arriving after the battles."

Matt grinned. "About time. Many of our other companies have known the fray."

Part of Richard agreed, but a chill beyond the bite of the cold wind passed through him. Their dismissal moved the men double-quick into introductions and easy banter with the almost legendary Texas Brigade troops.

Marc elbowed him. "Hey, why don't you ask the captain about their part in Second Manassas? I'd bet he'd tell you the details."

A young Texas soldier waited in front of them. He grinned. "You can try. The captain is particular 'bout stuff like that." He gave Matt a friendly shove. "I'll tell you about it if you help me unload that there wagon."

Matt's face brightened. "Sure."

John took Matt's place beside Richard. "It'll do him good to be with someone closer to his age."

"That boy's got a couple of years on Matt." Marc removed his hat. "But you're right."

"Excuse me, Lieutenant." The captain approached them, and all came to attention. The golden eyes narrowed, belied by a smile. "Relax, boys, we won't head out for a few days or so. The people in the town closest to us—Fredericksburg—are getting mighty nervous. They know Federal soldiers are headed to their town. You see those people over there by the far tent?"

Marc relaxed but didn't blink. "Yes, sir."

Without waiting for the others to respond, the captain continued. "Those are a few of the town residents trickling into camp. More are coming." He faced Marc. "I understand you're good with organizing and making efficient use of supplies and horses."

Richard smiled. "He is, sir, but he won't brag on himself."

Marc shifted. "Lots of our men will be happy to help those people. We haven't forgotten about our families at home."

The captain didn't smile. "Neither have we. Our families support us staying here until this war is over and we come home victorious."

Richard groaned inwardly; Marc had better use caution with his next words.

Marc smiled and reached out his hand. "Good. Where do you need me, Captain?"

The captain clasped his hand. "Follow me."

John heaved a sigh. "How did he manage that? I thought we'd have earned a reprimand."

Richard chuckled. "You're right, but it doesn't take long with Marc. We've always known he's skilled at whatever he takes a mind to learn. He cares and speaks plain."

"Yep, he gets the job done."

"Maybe I can ask one of the other Texans about Second Manassas."

A lanky man approached them. "Howdy, boys. Which part of Arkansas are you from?"

"Rockport—in Hot Spring County." Richard extended his hand.

The man shook it and then scratched his head. "It's close to the Ouachita River?"

"Yep."

"My cousin worked on a ferryboat there a couple of summers ago. He headed west when the war started."

The man seemed a good sort. Richard decided to like him. "Where are you from?"

"I live close to the Brazos River in Texas."

"What about Captain Richards? Is he part of the Eighteenth Georgia that's been with you?"

"No. He was originally from Georgia, but he and his wife and brother moved to East Texas before the war started. It's a little different story for him. He joined up with a friend of his who lives in another county in East Texas. Came with the First Texas Infantry."

Richard lifted his eyebrows when John smiled and leaned forward with his hand out. "Well, Brazos River. Guess we're the Third Texans now."

Their new friend grinned and shook John's hand. "I'm Frank Duncan."

John released his hand. "John Wilkins."

Richard removed his cap. "Richard Cushman."

"We've got a nice section all ready for your bedrolls. Let me show you."

Richard relaxed and followed Frank and John. If the man could get John talking, they'd found a new friend. He surveyed his other comrades joking and chatting with the Texans. These men understood brotherhood. He'd write Pa about them tonight.

While they divested themselves of their bedroll packs, which contained most of their limited goods rolled inside the tight blanket folds, Frank gave him a tempered description of Second Manassas. Part boast of how they'd "whipped them Federals," then followed by a silent somber moment of raw emotion as he recounted how Hood's men had lost hundreds from their own ranks. "We Rebs lost half of what they did." He spoke about a Lieutenant-Colonel Carter and Lieutenant-Colonel Gary, as well as other commanders Richard had not met at this point. Plus, he spoke about the leadership abilities of some they'd introduced today, including Brigadier General Robertson, General Longstreet, and General Hood.

Frank retold valor stories from comrades from the Eighteenth Georgia, Fifth Texas, Fourth Texas, and First Texas composing the Texas Brigade. He went on about an intense confrontation with some Federal troops from New York called the Zouaves.

Richard watched the intense display of excitement and sorrow dancing across the man's face. He glanced at John who leaned forward, transfixed.

"Private Duncan, you have duties beyond retelling Manassas—" Captain Richards joined them, "And I'll stop you before you start on Sharpsburg—Antietam."

Richard spoke before he thought. "That's not necessary. We were there."

The golden gaze narrowed. "Precisely. Look around, Private—"

"Cushman, sir—Richard Cushman."

Marc stepped from behind the captain. "These are tough fighters, sir."

"I want you to drill your company early in the morning. Give them a look at the troops building around us. Federals are setting up around the higher points near Fredericksburg. General Lee has his men, including us, gathered within two to five miles of the town. Stand at the ready."

Marc saluted. "Yes, sir."

Richard exhaled, watching the tall figure of the captain depart.

Frank patted him on the back. "You have him riled, but don't get him wrong. I met him early on equal footing. He'd return to private tomorrow if he could, but he does what's expected of him."

"What motivates him?"

"What motivates all of us? We believe in the cause and our ability to win. We wanted to come to Virginia to be in the toughest fights. We want to win and go home to our families, but we won't go on leaves until the war is done. You'll receive the same answer if you ask anyone in our brigade, but the captain is a bit different. He has a bitter taste in his mouth due to his uncle in Georgia. The man owns a huge plantation. Boyd—I mean Captain Richards—detests the system."

John stepped closer. "Then why didn't he fight for the Federals?"

"Oh, he loves the South minus slavery, but he loves his wife and newborn son more. He left Georgia and carved out his own life in Texas. Preserving his new life keeps him focused, but he retains a bit of a chip on his shoulder because his uncle refuses to leave him alone. Beside his exemplary record, his uncle made sure he got a commission. He's educated."

Marc cleared his throat. "You men sound like women around the washtub. More townspeople are trickling into camp." He moved closer. "I can't believe I'm ordering this, but from what I've learned, it's needed. Your rumored skills of finding provisions are necessary. These are hungry women and children arriving. Pass the word, John."

John disappeared.

"Richard, you come with me."

"How about me, Lieutenant?" Frank's face showed eagerness.

"Until we merge our ranks, you'd better check with your lieutenants."

Richard had no desire to move up the ranks. He liked being a private.

The tension of knowing the enemy moved along the high places surrounding them intensified the cold atmosphere. December and a tremendous battle awaited them. Richard shivered. He pulled his almost threadbare jacket closed and followed his lieutenant and friend.

The steady influx of townspeople continued over the next couple of chilly days. It wasn't long before he saw Matt tending to crying toddlers—their little lips tinged blue by the blustery wind. A few of the mothers and the older men evacuating the town appeared too weary to carry the children or forage enough to feed the empty bellies.

John and some other friends from their Arkansas ranks surrounded Marc. Richard joined them. A slight tug on his pants leg directed his gaze downward. A little girl of about three years of age blinked and then held her arms up to him. He swallowed hard. She reminded him of his youngest sister. Instinct beyond protocol took over—he scooped her up, and she laid her little head on his shoulder. Tears spurted to his eyes.

Marc cleared his throat. "I agree we can't let these people camp out in the cold. Your officers are well aware of the needs, but they need to focus on the threat of the build-up taking place on Stafford Heights above us. The murmur from within all our Arkansas companies has been heard. We will be building a bigger group shelter for the men of the town and some smaller ones for the women and little ones. By now, we're used to our harsh camp conditions, but *they* aren't. Let's move." Marc turned toward Richard. He studied the little girl and his eyes softened. "She looks a bit like Florey, doesn't she?"

Matt hurried over to them. "Let me take her, Richard. She grabbed me when they came into camp earlier. Her mother said her older brother is somewhere in this fray."

"Do you know where her mother is?" Richard relinquished the now sleeping child to him.

"Yes, she's over there with four more of her children."

Marc's jaw tightened. "Take her double-quick and hurry back here. We have work to do."

"Yes, sir."

Richard swiped the end of his cold nose and sniffed. "Makes you wonder what our families are facing right now, don't it?"

Marc's green eyes met his. An almost imperceptible nod followed. His childhood friend then resumed his lieutenant's mask, shuttering away his emotions. Richard followed him to where a sergeant was shouting orders and organizing the work detail.

Chapter Six

"Aww Hee Aww Oww . . ." The loud penetrating yell from the front room had Jenny covering her ears.

Mrs. Cushman hurried up the porch steps with Florey, Alice, and Dawn on her heels. Jenny hurried around the abandoned washtubs in the front yard, following the other girls.

Just as they opened the door, another yell reverberated from inside the house.

"Alan, what on earth?" Mrs. Cushman hurried toward Mr. Cushman. "Are you all right?"

Jenny peeked over Florey's shoulder. Mr. Cushman stood in front of the fireplace holding a letter. He looked up from the piece of paper, which had 'soldier mail' printed above the corner fold on the back. A grin appeared, and he grabbed Mrs. Cushman, whirling her around.

"Alan Cushman, you put me down this instant."

He complied, laughing. "Our gray-boys did it at Fredericksburg. Richard says he's never heard such military thunder and felt earthquaking vibrations like those. He says the Mississippi boys under Longstreet's Corp started the defense and shelled those Federals good. At first, they all thought the blue-boys had it. Richard said their numbers made his jaw drop."

Mrs. Cushman tried to take the letter from him. "Is our son hurt?"

Mr. Cushman shook his head. "They heard and saw it all but didn't have to engage."

Jenny let out the breath she'd been holding.

"Listen to this. '*Pa, I won't tell you all the details of our brave commanders, but I will say I'm proud to be part of Lee's troops. I just wish I had gotten to fire one shot. The Georgia boys from Stonewall's Second Corps did plenty for all of us, and our batteries finished the rest. Those early days of this festive month were the best gift any of us could have. Tell Ma, my sisters, and sweet Jenny I send my love.*'" Mr. Cushman glanced up and winked at her.

Jenny blushed, but Florey put her arm around her, giving her an affectionate squeeze. Dawn and Mrs. Cushman sent smiles her way.

Mr. Cushman laughed. "I'd better not read this next part to you, ladies."

Florey released Jenny and rushed forward. "Read it, Pa. Please?"

His eyes twinkled. "Here goes. '*Looks like they're gonna let us celebrate a bit for Christmas. They let our brigade build a theater and plan to have some music played too.*' Who'd have thought?"

Florey laughed. "Sounds like a right fine time."

Mrs. Cushman frowned. "It certainly does not. What would our pastor say?"

Mr. Cushman folded the letter. "I'd say he'd tell you even David rejoiced and played music after his battles in the Bible."

Ella Cushman rolled her eyes. "I don't think he built a theater." She turned. "It's getting late. We have wash to finish before it forms icicles." She pivoted toward her husband. "Please refrain from any more of that horrible yelling."

"Woman, that's our battle cry in the ranks."

"Kindly remember a few Federals might be hanging around these parts, and you don't want to invite them back to our farm. They stole a few pigs and chickens the last time they passed by."

In answer, Mr. Cushman put his hands on his hips and leaned back with his mouth open, "Aww Hee, Aww—"

Ella hurried toward him. "Shh—"

He grabbed her and kissed her. She gasped and pulled away, smoothing her hair.

Jenny ducked her chin, smiling. Florey elbowed her, then Dawn motioned them to follow her toward the door. They filed out onto the porch. Jenny couldn't help giggling as they went down the steps.

"Don't you two dare say anything to Ma. Let's finish the wash," Dawn said.

Jenny shivered against the cold breeze and grabbed the soap, applying it to the shirt she'd left on the washboard. "I'm just glad Richard is unharmed."

"I gather our other boys are also." Florey dunked a pair of soapy pants in the murky washtub's depths.

"Richard would have told us if they weren't, wouldn't he?"

Mrs. Cushman hurried down the steps, joining them. "I'm sure he would, daughter."

Jenny knew Florey's thoughts lingered on Matt, just as Dawn's pondered Marc Johnson's fate. She studied the youngest Cushman—eleven-year-old Alice—dipping a sock with lackadaisical enthusiasm. Jenny smiled.

"At least Alice doesn't have to worry about where her future beaus are at this moment. Will and Jack are just down the road."

A broad smile brightened the blonde-haired girl's face. "I'm well glad of it too. I just hope this war ends before one of them has to go because I haven't even decided which one I like the best."

Dawn grabbed the sock from her. "You're too young to be cow-eyed over boys. Besides, those two don't have any interest in you. You're as irritating a tagalong as Florey was to Marc, John, and Richard."

"I wasn't tagging along with them; I was following Matt."

Dawn lifted an eyebrow. "So you say."

Uh-oh. Those words might spark Florey's quick temper. Dawn should know better. Sure enough, Florey grabbed the wet pants out of the water and flung them at her older sister.

Dawn's quick, deflecting hands sent the wet garment to the dirt, but not without a spray of water drenching her skirt.

Mrs. Cushman moved in between her two daughters. "Young ladies, that is quite enough. You're creating more laundry instead of finishing it."

Jenny rubbed her arms. "It's getting colder. We'd better finish and hurry inside. None of us wants to get sick. We want to be here when our boys march home."

A somber silence ensued. Work resumed until completion.

Later that night, while darning socks and applying patches to ever-increasing threadbare garments, Jenny stared into the fire, thinking about her father. He had to come home. Missing her ma didn't get easier with time—she'd resigned herself to it. She'd never have her back this side of heaven, but Jenny longed to be home with her pa in their little cabin.

A soft touch on her shoulder shooed away her sad reverie. "I waited to give you this at day's end. It's a letter from your father." Mr. Cushman handed her the folded mail. "He and Richard must have posted theirs on the same day, or the mail wagons retrieved them together."

She tucked it inside the band of her skirt. "Thank you. I'll read it at bedtime."

He gazed out the window. "It appears to be about that time. The other girls have turned in for the night."

She looked to Mrs. Cushman knitting in the rocking chair. An affirming nod allowed her to place her sewing in the basket at her feet. "I'll finish tomorrow."

"Thank you, dear girl. I do hope you can influence Florence to pick up a needle to help you."

"Yes, ma'am." She smiled at her neighbors—now her host and hostess. "Good night." She lifted the small lantern on the table beside her. "May I take this to read by?"

Mr. Cushman turned from placing another log on the fire in the fireplace. "Of course, you may. Just don't forget to put out the flame before you sleep."

"I will." She crept toward the bed she shared with Alice in the room off the front of the house. Dawn and Florence slept in the bed across from theirs. After setting the lantern on the bedside table, she hurried to change into her gown before she caught a chill. When Alice groaned, Jenny turned the flame down a bit, grabbed the letter, and slid under the heavy quilt. Flipping on her left side to face the low flame, she unfolded the letter, squinting to read it in the dim light:

Dear Jenny,

I'm sure—I hope— Richard's letter has reached his parents. In order not to bore you with news twice told, I inquired about his retelling of the battle of Fredericksburg. Please have the Cushmans share it with you. Suffice it to say, it was a glorious and terrifying sight. We have the bravest of boys and men. However, it grieved my heart to assist in loading the fallen soldiers into wagons, but once done our hearts turned to light and victory, and we had a tremendous snowball fight within our ranks. Laughter is needed whenever we can find it these days. I do hope you find joy there at least once a day.

Jenny swiped at a tear. She couldn't imagine loading soldiers like a cord of wood. Tears fell from her eyes in earnest. She continued reading.

Don't lose faith, sweet daughter. Also, I do hope the farms there aren't picked bare by the soldiers passing through whether in gray or blue. I can't judge them too harshly as the farms near our camps have become lighter on our account.

Don't be too shocked, my dear. Soldiers must eat to have strength to fight, but in our scavenging, know that we don't take all we find. We remember our homes and try to help the people in the towns near us. I do believe the townspeople in Fredericksburg have appreciated the kindness our boys have shown them. In a way, it's like we're doing it for all of you at the same time.

The boundaries of foraging must blur for many during this war, but her Pa? Desperate times, she imagined, necessitated such things.

We never know what each day will bring us. I simply endeavor to do my duty and hope and pray it brings me home to my darling daughter. Sweet girl, I do have one request. If you can find a non-tattered shirt, please send it to me. War is worse than moths on clothes.

Write when you can. You have my permission to include a few lines for me to share with Richard if you have the inclination. May the Good Lord keep you.

Your Pa

As desperate as it might be to find any cloth to sew or solid clothing, she'd mend or make him a shirt. She folded the letter and placed it under her pillow.

Dear Lord,

I don't know the rights and wrongs of this war in your eyes, but I do know the hearts of our Rockport soldiers. Please watch over them and all our boys in gray and especially my pa.

Amen

She blew out the lantern flame and turned down the wick.

A chill caused her teeth to chatter, and she swiped the tip of her cold nose, pulling up the quilt to her neck. What lines should she include for Richard in her next letter to Pa? Richard . . . Oh, how could she forget? *Dear God, please protect Richard.*

Jenny listened to the easy breathing of Alice beside her, willing herself to sleep. A yawn overtook her. She'd seen a temporary encampment of soldiers near the river last month. What a scary thing it must be to camp outdoors with the enemy nearby and little protection from the cold. That reminded her; she'd start sewing shirts to send them tomorrow.

Chapter Seven

"Pickett's men will leave us now. They will camp north of Richmond." The general held his mount steady with his leather gauntlet-covered hands. "We will camp to the south of town. This is a busy city. The quartermaster has moved a few things from our warehouse here, so, I have surprises for you once we set up camp."

Richard fingered a hole in the shirt Jenny had sent him in early January.

A deep chuckle from the general lifted his gaze, as well as his fellow soldiers'. "Captains, you'd best double-time your men to Petersburg Pike. The sights of this fair city are distracting them a mite."

Several of his fellow soldiers gaped at two lovely ladies dressed in less-than-refined attire, smiling brazenly at the troops from in front of a large tavern. Richard elbowed John and whispered, "You'd better close Matt's and Bevil's mouths before the February breeze freezes them that way." John elbowed his younger brother and his young Texas friend.

"Men, you heard the general. Let's get to camp double quick." Captain Boyd Richards and the other officers led all their companies out of the tantalizing city.

Richard had to admit the busy town had an energy he'd never felt before. The sprawling city blocks and tall buildings amazed him. He wouldn't have minded relishing the sights longer than a march-through allowed, but for him, that didn't include the offerings of those fair ladies. His heart belonged to only one young woman—if she'd have him one day.

After a fast-paced march, they arrived at the campsite. Several wagons waited for them, surrounded by a few troops who'd gone on ahead of them. Each man wore a broad smile—welcoming but withholding the secret of the wagons' contents. The generals rode to the front. Brigadier General Robertson, their brigade commander, received a nod from Major General Hood, their division commander. He removed his hat.

"Gentlemen, it gives me great pleasure to reward your perseverance, loyalty, and sacrifice. These wagons hold what we have long done without—food and new clothing."

A contagion of whoops filtered through the ranks. The general held up his hand. "Once we complete the setup of a bivouac here, the garments will be issued to each man." He cleared his throat. "General Hood also has planned another reward for you, but I must say we all are not in agreement, especially myself and Colonel Manning. He assures me, however, it will do you good and improve your morale for the coming battles." He stroked his dark beard and then smoothed his mustache. "You gentlemen will have passes to enjoy evenings in the fair city of Richmond."

The expected shouts did not erupt. Richard glanced around. A few tentative grins twitched the lips of his fellow soldiers, but they held back, as if waiting for a condition from the career soldier addressing them. Fortunately, it didn't come. General Robertson placed his hat on his head and turned his horse, heading for the tent his aide and a few soldiers had erected for him.

General Hood tipped his hat and reined his horse in the same direction as his fellow officer. Colonel Manning, now recovered from the wounds he'd received at Sharpsburg, dismissed them to their duties.

The men milled around a bit, the buzz of conversation filtering evening plans.

Matt hurried up to Richard. "Hey, you going into town when they give us those passes?" He peeked back over his shoulder at Bevil Henry who never seemed to stray too far from him. "Bevil and I want to go."

Richard sighed. "I haven't decided. Did you ask John?"

"Why would I ask him? Pa's here, but he said he isn't going into town. Besides, the generals said it's good for morale."

John joined them. "We need to set up the tents. Do you think they'll let us go into Richmond tonight or tomorrow night?"

Matt grinned.

Richard quirked an eyebrow. "It seems the Wilkins brothers are ready for town."

John's serious gaze turned on his younger brother and his friend. "I knew you two whelps wanted to go.

Pa told me. I'm not letting you go without me. No offense, Bevil, but you're liable to get Matt into trouble without me there."

Bevil twisted his mouth and then popped his lips. "More than likely."

They all laughed.

Richard shook his head. "We'd better get to work. I'm more concerned about getting some new clothes than going to town. In case you hadn't noticed, it's cold."

Bevil untucked the tattered tail of his shirt. "Don't I know it." He adjusted his cylindrical bedroll pack slung across his chest from his shoulder to his waist. "Let's earn our rewards."

Close to sunset, the men, now adorned in new issues of clothing and shoes, headed back into Richmond. All they lacked were new hats, but the quartermaster shook his head at all who'd inquired. General Hood and a few of the officers rode with them. Word had trickled down that they'd received invitations to parties at some of the finest homes in Richmond.

General Robertson and Colonel Manning remained in camp. Richard and a handful of men also stayed behind.

Richard sidled up to Mr. Wilkins and Jenny's pa. "You sure you don't want to see the city's offerings?"

Jenny's father gave him a warm smile. "No, son. Before I married Jenny's ma, I lived the life of a mountain man. I'm not too fond of cities. Our small river town at home is enough." He placed a hand on his shoulder. "I'm pleased you decided to stay in camp. Does it have anything to do with my daughter?"

Richard ducked his head when heat crept up his neck and cheeks. He took a moment and then smiled up at the man he hoped would be his father-in-law. "It has everything to do with her."

The man patted his shoulder. "That's fine. Right fine, my boy."

Mr. Wilkins nodded at him. "I just hope John can keep those two young ruffians in line."

Marc joined them and waved their salutes away. "Matt is too crazy about Florey to stray too far."

Richard gave a little whistle. "He's young, and Bevil holds strong influence."

"Hmpf." Mr. Wilkins spat on the ground. "That's why John went. Still, it's good for the boys to have a little fun. I hear Richmond has more than one thing to offer. Those boys need to be reminded about life outside of war." He lifted an eyebrow. "If I might ask, Lieutenant Johnson, why aren't you going to town?"

"Captain Richards and I have invitations to a dinner at a fine home tomorrow night, but we prefer the quiet of the camp tonight. Would you gentlemen care to eat with us? The cooks have prepared something with the new supplies."

Richard liked seeing his friend relax and relate to them as he used to do. "Thank you for the invitation. I accept."

The older men, both corporals, requested permission to take a plate to their tents, saying they had letters to write.

Richard followed Marc to a campfire outside of Captain Richards's canvas tent.

The golden-haired officer sat on an overturned stump. "Good evening. I'm glad you could join us,

Private." He smiled and then held up one finger. "Wait. For tonight, I give each of us a reprieve. No ranks. For conversation's sake, if you address me, you may call me Boyd or nothing at all. It's my furlough for the three of us tonight."

Richard relaxed. "That's welcome. Thank you."

Two of the cooks hurried over with their plates— no corn dodgers or snitched Yankee hardtack and maggots tonight—cornbread, cooked bacon, and beans. A third man brought them cups of real coffee.

Richard inhaled the aroma and took a tentative sip of the steaming liquid. "It's been a bit." Warmth spread from the heat of the tin cup in his hands throughout his body through the fortifying liquid he sipped. "I won't let this get cold. I'll chase my food with water."

Marc and Boyd laughed.

Richard took another sip, studying Captain Richards—Boyd—over the rim of the cup. "I understand you're married and have a baby son."

"I do. Her name is Nancy, and his name is Sam—I haven't met him yet, but she's written me about him." He looked down. "It was the hardest thing to leave her in such a delicate condition, but Ben, my younger brother, is there with them. He's about Bevil's age and a great artist." The captain stood and ducked into his tent, returning with a piece of paper. He extended it to Richard.

Richard set his coffee cup and plate on the ground and then took the paper. He scooted close enough to the campfire to illuminate the sketch. A woman with dark, windswept hair and laughing eyes stood overlooking a grassy field. The details were so vivid Richard could almost feel the wind and smell the rich farmland. Boyd's wife radiated warmth of character.

He couldn't help but smile. "I don't know much about art, but your brother's work rivals what I've seen. He could be sketching like those artists who follow us around on the battlefields." Richard handed the paper to Marc.

Marc nodded. "I've seen it and agree." He passed it to Boyd. "I'd love to meet Boyd's family after the war."

"It's clear you two have gotten to know each other." Richard dispelled the slight jealousy of sharing his best friend and grinned. "Officers can do that."

The fire reflected in Boyd's eyes, deepening them to amber. "I'd like to get to know a bit more about you, Mr. Cushman. With all the dying, it's sometimes easier to keep your distance, but sometimes it's not."

Richard took a deep breath. "Yep. What hasn't Marc told you about Rockport?"

Marc laughed.

Boyd joined him. "Guess I do know more about you than I thought, but he tells me you have honorable intentions towards a young lady there. As her father is one of our troops, why don't you tell me a bit more."

Richard's heart raced. Why had Marc told Captain Richards about Jenny? He shot Marc a look his friend knew well. Marc had the decency to duck his head. Richard returned his attention to the officer trying to befriend him. "As I've not yet asked for her hand, I'll withhold speaking of my feelings until I share them with the young lady, but I will say my heart has wanted to protect her from the first time we met in the schoolyard. You've met her father, but you'll never know her dignified Indian mother." He waited, but the captain's expression remained the same. "Jenny has experienced loss, but I won't try to explain her. I don't have to. Let's just say I could write a better song about her than all the songs the men have been singing so far."

Boyd crossed his arms. "Do you write songs?"

Richard chuckled. "No, but my heart sure sings every time I think of her."

The captain slapped him on the shoulder. "Enough said. I understand your sentiment. Excuse me." He ducked back into the tent with the sketch and returned with three blankets. "The wind is stirring. These new blankets are rare." He handed one to Richard and Marc and then wrapped the third one around his own shoulders.

Richard followed suit. "I understand you grew up on a big plantation in Georgia."

Marc took in an audible breath and shook his head. The captain smirked.

"It's fine, Marc." He turned back toward Richard and sat on the overturned stump across from him, picking up his plate of food. "I did." He took a bite, chewed, and swallowed. "I don't care to discuss it much." He took a sip of coffee. "My parents both died, and my aunt and uncle raised us. I agree with fighting for state's rights but am against slavery." He bit off a piece of bacon. "Many men within this brigade feel differently. That's their right. I own my own farm now and want to plant the crops I choose and raise the livestock I choose without the government's interference. The South should have the right to do that"—He shrugged—"but my uncle is a hard man. My brother and I grew up with children born into slavery. Two of our best friends are still there. That's all I'll say."

Richard swallowed hard at the challenge in Captain Boyd Richards's eyes. "Enough said." He cleared his throat. "Tell me about your plans for your farm. Marc's and my families are farmers. That's what I want to be."

The conversation turned to crops, soil, and weather. They even broke out a deck of cards and played a few hands.

An unmistakable song lamenting home and the girl left behind echoed out of the darkness a couple of hours later. The men returning to camp slurred and laughed their way through a poor rendition. The soldiers on picket duty greeted them with laughter.

Boyd stood. "As most of the commanders and officers are dining at an esteemed home in Richmond tonight, I need to see if Colonel Manning has retired for the evening or has instructions for me on settling these men." He stroked his beard. "I won't disturb General Robertson."

Richard turned and Marc rushed past him, catching Bevil before he hit the ground. John hoisted an arm around Matt who grinned like a silly schoolgirl. The boy put a finger to his lips. "Don't tell Pa. I thought it were coffee, but Bevil tipped some whiskey in it. Right, John?"

John scooped up his brother. "Yep, and he was quite sly about it." He nodded at Marc. "Put Bevil in bed before I dunk his head in cold water—If you please, Lieutenant Johnson."

Richard chuckled. Tonight held no military ranks, but they'd be firmly reinstated in the morning. No doubt, drills and marches awaited them before first light. He helped Marc pull Bevil to his feet. They flanked him, supporting him under his arms, and navigated him to the two-sided tent holding his bedroll.

The sound of retching right outside ceased, and John deposited Matt on the blanket beside Bevil's, "That sly Texan outwitted me, boys."

Richard straightened and patted John on the shoulder. "Matt had to learn some time."

John grunted. "If Miss Florence Cushman could see him now."

Matt groaned, opening one eye. "Florey." He opened his arms wide. "The most beautiful girl." He sat up. "Don't you think so, Marc?"

Marc extricated himself from Bevil's flailing arms. "Sure thing, Matt, but she does have freckles on her nose."

What? Richard peered at his best friend. Since when had he noticed anything about his middle sister? He shrugged.

Marc stood, joining him and John. "Let's turn in. You men have early drills in the morning."

The old friend faded, and the lieutenant returned to his position.

Richard heaved a breath—at least *his* head would be clear for the drills. He took one last look at the now snoozing youths and grinned. They would pay for their evening of folly. He said a prayer for them. At least Matt's experience hadn't been intentional.

Chapter Eight

The late May breeze proclaimed summer. Jenny lifted her face, relishing the warm wind even more than the cooler ones heralding spring. She loved summer. Florey said Jenny was crazy, since Florey preferred late winter and early spring planting to harvesting time. This year the sparse crops promised a limited return. Jenny enjoyed harvesting the most. Gathering the results of their work satisfied her. She didn't mind picking cotton, digging potatoes, or shelling peas. The men picked the watermelons.

The leaves in the tree above her head shook when a shot sounded. Jenny dropped to a crouch. Young Jack Johnson sprang from the tree. She grabbed his arm, pulling him down beside her.

The tree shook again when another shot reverberated through the air.

"Tarnation," Jack whispered. "I need to get back in that tree. Alice and Florey are still up there. I went low, thinking they'd follow."

What? What in the world are they doing? She'd bet anything Florey had talked Alice into climbing the tree. "Wait. Where's Will?"

Jack rolled his eyes. "You know *he* ain't up there. Don't you remember the branch breaking on him last time?"

Jenny frowned. "No."

Jack shook off her arm. "Don't matter. Those shots aren't friendly. 'Sides, Will's helping Pa cut timber."

Jenny peeked back at the porch. Mrs. Cushman had gone over early to tend Mrs.Wilkins, their sick neighbor. With Mr. Cushman gone to town, only Dawn remained in the house. The curtain over the front room window stirred. Jenny shook her head, hoping Dawn could see her.

The leaves above them stopped moving, but no one fell from the tree. Jenny exhaled. Jack dashed around the side of the house, leaving her alone in the yard. Another shot sounded, followed by distinctive hoofbeats. Her heart pounded. She lifted her head. A shabby rider reined his horse and dismounted, holding his shotgun.

"Well, look what we have here—a squaw-girl." He grinned, revealing yellow teeth.

Jenny rose. She wouldn't cower.

The stranger circled her. She lifted her chin. He laughed.

"I knew I picked the right road today."

She met his disgusting gaze. "I didn't think soldiers picked their own roads."

"I'm not exactly a soldier." His gaze narrowed. "If and when I choose to be, I pick the side that suits me best." He shifted his gun under his arm and scratched his head, tilting his face upward. "I could have sworn a varmint was still in that tree after the boy jumped down." He glanced at the tree base.

Florey had obviously taken Alice higher, hiding in the thicker foliage of the left side closer to the house. They'd hidden up there once before. No one could see them from the road or house. The boys hadn't found them in their younger days. It had been funny then. She swallowed hard, lifting a silent prayer.

The stranger frowned and snickered. "Maybe I should shoot up there one more time."

"I wouldn't do that."

Jenny whirled around at the sound of Mr. Cushman's firm voice. So did the stranger, shotgun in hand. A shot rang out before the vile man could fire. His shoulder recoiled, blood spurting toward her. The shotgun fell from his hands. He stumbled backward, falling to the ground.

Before Jenny could move, Mr. Johnson rushed from the back of the barn and kicked the stranger's gun out of reach. Mr. Cushman hobbled forward from the side of the house—his gun leveled at the man on the ground.

"Get up."

The man glared at him.

"Let me assist you." Mr. Johnson hauled the wounded man to his feet, ignoring his grunts and bloodied condition. "Jack, bring me some rope."

Jack and Will appeared from the barn.

Once Mr. Johnson had trussed the man's hands and legs tighter than a turkey, he nodded at Mr. Cushman.

"Girls, get down here." Mr. Cushman didn't even look upward.

A small shower of twigs and leaves preceded the careful descent of what appeared to be two boys. Given the seriousness of the situation, Jenny suppressed the giggle about to erupt.

The stranger had no such inclination. He snickered. "Girls? Someone needs to tan their hides. I thought they were sharpshooters hiding up there."

Will rushed to Alice's side. "She's hit!" He spun around and knocked the stranger to the ground.

The trussed-up man moaned.

Will hovered over him, his stocky almost fourteen-year-old frame rigid with rage.

Florey put her arm around her little sister. "It just grazed her."

Jack turned toward the house when Dawn came rushing down the front steps. Alice burst out crying. Florey paled, the day having taken its toll on her. The men could deal with the rest.

Dawn pulled her youngest sister close and hurried toward the house.

Jenny took Florey by the hand. "Let's go inside." For once, her friend didn't have anything to say.

The stranger cackled behind Jenny. "You've got a strange group here. That pretty blonde is the only lady I've seen on the place." Mr. Cushman and Mr. Johnson jerked him to his feet.

Jenny hurried Florey inside.

Dawn had grabbed her mother's basket of sewing scraps used for bandages. She lifted the kettle hanging over the fire and poured hot, steaming water into a stone bowl. "Jenny, take her shirt off, please. Florey, go get that bottle of reddish liquid Pa brought home from the war. He said the surgeon used it on him to clean and heal—something about preventing infection."

Tears coursed down Alice's face as Jenny took care peeling the shirt away. "Poor Richard won't have any clothes when he comes home if you two don't quit borrowing them."

Alice swiped at her cheeks with the back of her hand. "It's only the second time I've done it." She eyed her bloodied left upper arm, and her bottom lip trembled. Her eyes searched Jenny's. "I'm not going to lose my arm, am I?"

Jenny placed a strip of cloth in the hot water. "Florey said it only grazed you, so you'll be fine, but we need to clean it." She stood. "I'm going to go grab my ma's bag of herbs. Your sisters can clean it however they like, but I know the Indian ways. We'll heal it." Jenny didn't wait for permission. Instead, she dashed out the door, ignoring the departing horses. She didn't dare draw attention. Apprehension and adrenaline coursed through her. Taking the wooded path to her house, she reached it without meeting anyone.

The lonely cabin still felt like home and safety. Jenny lifted the latch and pushed open the wooden door. The temptation to linger danced in her stomach. *No*! She had to hurry back. Grabbing the wooden box from the mantel, she slid open the top. A woodsy aroma tickled her nostrils. Assured the soft, deerskin pouch still lay within, she slid the box closed again. Clutching it to her chest, she took one last look at the forlorn room and then hurried to the door.

Mrs. Cushman had arrived and taken over by the time she returned.

Sweat trickled from Jenny's hairline. She swiped a strand away and bent over, trying to catch her breath.

"Goodness sakes, Jenny. Why have you been running?"

"I . . . I . . . brought my ma's herbs to doctor Alice."

Mrs. Cushman didn't scoff but still shook her head. "It's cleaned, doctored, and bandaged for now. But"—she took the box from Jenny—"we may need these when we change the dressing tonight. Your mother had healing ways indeed."

Love for their sweet neighbor washed over Jenny. She smiled.

Dawn finished pulling Alice's gown over her head, then put her uninjured arm in a sleeve. She tied the loose one in a knot and left it hanging.

The front door opened. Mr. Cushman stepped inside.

Alice frowned. "I look like a soldier with one arm."

Florey flounced into the chair beside her. "You almost were."

Mr. Cushman closed the door behind him and crossed his arms. "You're right. She was."

Florey straightened and looked ready to run. "I'm sorry, Pa. We didn't know that man was on the road."

Even injured, Alice defended her sister. "That's right, Pa. We were just climbing to see the birds closer."

The thunderous mask on Mr. Cushman's face slipped a bit. "To see the . . . I'll bet every one of them flew away."

Alice laughed. "How'd you know?"

Jenny slid onto a chair, tucked her hands under her legs, and straightened her back to prevent fidgeting. Would he laugh? She hoped not.

Mr. Cushman closed his eyes and leaned back against the door. "Florence Elizabeth Cushman, come here."

Florey obeyed. "I'm here."

Jenny met Mrs. Cushman's eyes. Her hostess placed a finger to her lips and encompassed Alice in her warning gaze. All eyes shifted toward the door, waiting for Mr. Cushman to speak.

His eyes opened, looking straight at Florey and no one else. "I have tried to understand your adventurous spirit. Your ma explained why you first donned your brother's clothes after the war started. After I returned home, it seemed practical and safer at the time. You could help me with your brother's old chores and run to our neighbors' or to town without drawing attention. Strangers passing through only saw a young boy—or so they thought. But things change, and you are getting older, the war is getting longer, men are getting meaner, and"—he heaved his breath—"I never said Alice could do what we allowed you to do." He stepped away from the door. "You are never to ask Alice, Jenny, or Dawn—"

Dawn gasped. "Pa, I would never—"

Mr. Cushman spared his eldest daughter a quick glance. "No, I suppose you wouldn't." His regard returned to Florey. "Do you understand me?"

Florey dropped her head. "Yes, sir. I never meant for Alice to get hurt."

Mr. Cushman lifted her chin. "Understood, but I'm not just talking about her. I don't want you to get hurt either." He sighed and walked to the fireplace. "The stranger was right about one thing. Sharpshooters are often found in trees." He turned toward them. "I even climbed one with your brother under orders."

Jenny's eyes widened as much as Alice's. Did her face register as much shock as Dawn's and Mrs. Cushman's faces?

No one spoke. Mr. Cushman continued. "I forbid anymore tree climbing until this war is over." His eyes darted from one to the other. "Understood?"

Alice touched her bandage. "Yes, sir."

Jenny nodded. "Yes, Mr. Cushman."

Florence swiped at the dust on the dirty trousers she wore. "Yes, Pa."

Mr. Cushman gave Florey a quick hug. "You can still wear these clothes for chores when I'm with you, but no more running around in them. You're becoming a young lady. And, Jenny"—he tilted his head toward her—"I've heard you keep running back to your house. You ask permission before going. I don't want you going alone."

Jenny's stomach churned. "Yes, sir." She stood. "Have you heard from Richard? I haven't had a letter from my pa in a bit."

"I imagine you haven't." Mr. Cushman paused. "We haven't had one either, but Mr. Johnson received one from Marc yesterday. The Third lost some men from Company C coming back from a canceled operation at Fort Hughes. None from our Company F, but it looks like the boys had a lively April. Hood and Colonel Manning selected the Third for some action—a few night operations involving their sharpshooting and covert skills." He bowed his head. "A couple of our company members did die. Mr. Johnson said he wouldn't share the names until he checked with the families to see if they'd been notified. The papers often tell us before the letters reach us anymore."

Jenny gasped.

He held up his hand. "Richard, Marc, John, and Matt are fine. They went back to Richmond the first week of this month. Some of the boys had their photographs taken." He glanced at Mrs. Cushman. "I hope they'll send those images home." He stroked his mustache. "Anyway, the Third marched as a detachment to guard one of the railroads, while the Texans marched onward." He grinned. "In fact, they made the Third Infantry into the Third Arkansas Mounted Infantry about mid-month. Marc is lark happy, but they've had to make some adjustments."

Florey's somber face brightened. "I know he's happy. He's mighty good on a horse."

Jenny joined in, relief coursing through her. "My pa also loves the horses."

Mr. Cushman squinted and nodded. "Hm, that's true, but fighting from a horse is an acquired skill none of them have. At least riding on a horse beats walking all those miles."

"Did Marc's letter give any more news?"

"Not much. They are all saddened about the death of Stonewall Jackson. Mr. Johnson says Marc asked more about how everyone was doing here at home. He did allow the Mounted Infantry situation doesn't appear to be permanent."

Mrs. Cushman stood, her mouth in a firm line. "Jenny, Dawn, you come help me with supper. Florey, you change your clothes and sit with Alice."

Mr. Cushman strode to the door. "Ella, a word, please."

Mrs. Cushman nodded. "Girls, set the table."

No one moved. They all knew voices carried from the porch if they kept quiet. None of them disallowed eavesdropping.

Mr. Cushman's voice carried well enough. "Town's near deserted, but we happened on a captain from one of our units in gray. They're encamped a few miles from town. The officers will decide the fate of the man who shot at the girls and assaulted Jenny."

While Mrs. Cushman's soft response didn't reach them, the voice of Mr. Cushman did. "Don't try to keep those groups straight, my dear. Bushwhackers are on our side most of the time, but they are way north of here close to the Missouri line. Guerrillas can be on either side."

Jenny didn't want to hear any more. She retrieved the plates. Dawn joined her. They worked in silence until the door opened, and Mrs. Cushman hurried toward her.

"Jenny, forgive me. Let me look you over." She gasped. "You have blood on your dress."

"It's the stranger's, not mine."

"We've taken on so about Alice and forgot about your ordeal today."

"I'm fine."

"Even so, you go change your dress and rest. Dawn and I will prepare the food."

No, she didn't want to rest or be alone. "Please, let me change my clothes and help."

"Are you sure?"

"Yes, ma'am."

She didn't want time to think about today. None of them wanted another stranger on the place, but none of them could control this war or all the changes it brought with it. Part of her wished she had Florey's gumption. She'd grab a horse and go find her father. Instead, Jenny headed for the bedroom. The secure boundaries of home held most women, but many of their neighbors had crossed those now unsecured lines and fled to Texas for safety. Who knew if they'd return after the war? Jenny grabbed a pillow from the bed and screamed into it. This war knew no boundaries. Tears coursed down her face.

Chapter Nine

Gettysburg July 2, 1863

"Shoulder arms! Move out!" came the command upon completion of the inspection of their gear.

Richard swallowed hard and sent a silent prayer toward the predawn sky. He calculated their steps and figured they'd marched about five or six miles when they halted. The sun rose and the heat dawned with the sunrise. Their artillery passed by, and they waited. Part of their division—General Hood's—waited in a field west of Herr's Ridge and Chambersburg Road with McLaws' Division. Law's Brigade had not yet arrived.

Cannon fire sounded in the distance. Sweat trickled down Richard's face and neck as the wait lengthened. The sun crested high overhead. His stomach rumbled, but the commanders had more important things than food on their minds.

Marc approached him.

Richard straightened. "Yes, sir?"

Marc waved away his salute. "General Law's Brigade has arrived." He nodded toward a group of men. "They've marched a ways. We'll let them rest a bit and then be ready."

Richard noted the exhausted state of the weary men. Some slumped to the ground, sitting with arms propped on their knees or their heads leaned against their muskets. From the looks of the men, they needed more than a brief rest. All the brigades within Hood's Division were to take part in the battle today. Apprehension and excitement danced within his belly at the thought. Even with their actions of late, today felt different. John had said it best last night. "Battle is rumbling like hunger pains. We'll satisfy it tomorrow."

He nodded toward John, Matt, and Bevil. "Do you think they're ready?"

Marc didn't grin. "Are you?"

A spark of irritation brought a frown. "I'm as ready as you are, but does it matter?"

"No." Marc removed his hat. His green eyes held a somber light. "We've seen plenty of men die before, but I just walked to the top of that ridge and looked at the terrain. Many more men will die today. We might be among them." His jaw clenched, and he glanced to his right. "From what Longstreet has shared with General Robertson, and Colonel Manning has shared with me, Lee's plans are specific. We must win and then go on to take Washington."

Richard released a soft whistle. "So, today could determine the war?"

Marc combed back his hair with his fingers. "I'll be surprised if this battle is over in one day." He replaced his hat on his head. "The report from yesterday's action is—" He pointed. "You can't see it as well from over here as I did from over there, but there are lots of ridges and hills. Our generals stood on Seminary Ridge last night, planning for today. From what I could see, there are other ridges—Cemetery Ridge, Houck's Ridge, and two bigger hills, the Round Tops. We'll march toward them today. There are a couple of more hills we can't see from here. Whoever takes them has the advantage. We don't know how long this battle will last. They tell me the numbers are more than most can fathom."

Marc had become closed-lipped, his rank impacting what he discussed. Richard frowned. "Why are you telling me this?"

Marc crossed his arms. "You're my best friend, Richard. I want you to be prepared. Follow orders, move fast, and keep moving—survive it."

Captain Boyd Richards strode over from the vicinity of the rest of the First Texas. "Emmitsburg Road."

Marc nodded, and Captain Richards moved away. Richard had come to respect the tall man with the golden eyes.

"Fall in." Marc slapped Richard on the shoulder. Richard coughed and moved into the forming file, obeying the orders his friend shouted.

McLaws' Division filed ahead of Hood's. They marched and marched.

A sudden halt stalled their progress. They waited. Richard couldn't see the cause of the delay, but he followed Longstreet and McLaws' new commands. After McLaws' men reversed direction, orders directed both divisions on a longer route to keep from being spotted by the Yanks.

It seemed to take forever, but they moved along and finally reached the cover of trees upon another ridge murmured to be across from a peach orchard, close to the Emmitsburg Road. In front of them, McLaws' men started forward, leaving the shadows of the trees.

Richard bumped into the man in front of him. Once again, they'd stopped. Like dominoes, the rest halted. He could hear the twinge of frustration in the murmurs within the ranks.

The officers conferred. Then Marc spoke two words, "Federals ahead."

None had planned on the Yanks being in the peach orchard ahead of them. How could they reach the Emmitsburg Road without being seen?

Their division split off from McLaws' Division, moving to the right of them. Law's Alabama Brigade became the spearhead and then the Texas Brigade, with the Georgians behind them. They moved into position by late mid-afternoon.

"Halt!" Law's men moved to the right. Orders came for Hood's men to move to the left of them, guarding Law's flank.

Colonel Manning ordered the Third Arkansas to the left of the First Texas, who stood in position to the left of the Fourth and Fifth Texas. The Georgians took positions at the rear.

Richard scanned their surroundings—a wooded area near the targeted road. He could smell the fields and trees. The two rising hills within his range of sight chilled him. The glint of artillery and guns reflected above them.

Trepidation filled Richard. He'd never seen such a sight. His insides quaked. Artillery exploded before he could finish his perusal of the topography ahead of him.

General Hood and General Longstreet urged their horses forward past their lines. Orders commenced. Their lines spread out—Richard and the rest of the Third Arkansas followed Colonel Manning's orders and moved far left of the others. He could still see some of the men from the First Texas to his right, but he had no idea where the Fourth and Fifth Texas and Law's Brigade had landed. Artillery sounded again, and canister shots started to fly. They must be firing two at a time.

General Robertson's voice, followed by their captain's command focused Richard. "Men, hit the dirt."

Richard dove for the ground, keeping his head low. Colonel Manning moved amongst them, speaking in a calm voice. Most stayed low, but a couple of young privates had trouble staying down. Their captains pulled them to the ground. Minié-balls, grapeshot, and canister shot whizzed forward. Some bounced, but many found their targets. Dirt sprayed his face. He spit and lowered his head to the earth beneath him.

A sickening pop and squishing sound came from the left. One of his childhood classmates balled up next to him, clutching a dismembered hand. Moans erupted amidst sprays of dust, smoke, and blood. General Robertson called them to action, warning them to remove a fence line ahead of them.

Colonel Manning ordered them to their feet. Richard moved forward with the rest in the direction of the colonel's raised sword directing them.

They left the cover of the trees in Biesecker's Woods on Warfield's Ridge, surged down the slope, and crossed the road, removing and toppling the wooden fence in their path. Matt surged forward next to him. The Federals' artillery—on one side from the direction of the peach orchard—and fire from Union sharpshooters dead ahead of them kept them moving. More artillery rained on them from one of the hills.

As they crossed the farmland, a short stone wall blocked them. Two of their boys in front of Richard fell before climbing over it, and he had to step over them. When Matt hesitated, Richard elbowed him and climbed over the small rock wall. Matt followed.

Richard squinted to his right. He spotted Captain Richards—the First Texas—but where were the Fourth and Fifth? Why was there a gap in their lines?

Smoke obscured his vision. Richard coughed and moved through it. He spotted a house in the distance, a reminder he needed. People lived here. Before the troops arrived, these rolling hills, these farms meant home for the owners.

Stop thinking. Move.

He surged ahead. His worn shoes squished in a patch of wet, muddy grass. The summer heat intensified. Richard's dry mouth and throat cried for moisture. The clank of his close-to-empty canteen mocked him. He should have sent it with the canteen bearers to refill. What did it matter? He kept his eyes trained ahead.

A wooded area lay to the left on one side, and the field continued on the other. The Arkansas companies angled into the right-southern side of the woods on their left. Except for the ranks of men nearest his right side, the rest of the First Texas continued plodding in the ever-changing, rough terrain of the field next to them.

Richard tried to catch his breath, relishing the shade and cover of the trees. Sweat beaded on his brow and trickled into his eyes. He swiped it away.

A few seconds later, he wished for the field, as they dodged bullets and artillery from the left and front, picking their way through the trees and boggy ground. Men fell all around him. He stopped and reloaded. The sequence in loading his rifle had become automatic—grabbing a cartridge from his box, tearing the paper with his teeth, pouring in the powder, inserting the minié ball, ramming it in the barrel of his musket-rifle, returning the ramrod, half-cocking the hammer, placing a musket cap, and pulling the hammer to full-ready. He figured he could load and shoot three times in a minute.

Colonel Manning shouted orders, but none of them could hear him. Their leader pointed ahead, guiding them. They fell back at his signal. A few moments later, they advanced again.

Would he ever leave Rose Woods or be carried out? One thing Richard knew, he'd clear as many Federals as possible.

A line of huge boulders lay close to the edge of the woods to his right. They used them as cover. He reloaded, searching for their leaders. After a quick scan, he located Colonel Manning behind the big rocks with blood pouring from his forehead and across his nose. Two soldiers tended him.

The intense artillery attacks and sound of infantry guns exploded in the now rocky field beside them. He glanced to his right, but an explosion of fire behind him drew his attention. He threw back his head and yelled. Others in the Third joined him. The fighting intensified.

Another brigade in gray came from the left, Georgians providing relief on their left flank.

They emerged from the trees. The remainder of the First Texas knelt behind a stone-wall fence. He joined them. What an odd field beyond them—two other stone-wall fences angled from the edge of their barrier, meeting at a corner, making the field a triangle.

Richard ducked, grateful for the cover. Bevil, Matt's best friend from the First Texas, fired his gun, reloaded, and turned to him.

"Their cannons couldn't reach us when it sloped back there. They can't reach us. We're too low for them." He grinned. "Let's do some shooting."

Half of the Texans stood, and the ones kneeling behind the wall squeezed off a barrage toward the Federal battery on the ridge above them. Even though the cannons couldn't reach them, the Union boys kept answering them with artillery.

They received orders to spread out their line. Richard refused to look back. Matt appeared to his left. *Forward. Fall back.*

Matt screamed and squatted. John lay on the ground in front of him. Richard moved toward them.

John gasped. "Get Matt out of here, Richard."

In a moment, Marc appeared at his left elbow, and Captain Richards dashed in from the right.

"Fall back, boys." Marc's command broached no argument.

To their right, the First Texans and the rest of the Third complied. Richard grabbed Matt's arm and pulled him along with him to the rock wall.

He glanced back in time to see Marc and the captain pull John behind a cluster of trees and rocks. Yelling voices behind them alerted him to the movement of some more Georgian troops joining the First Texas. Lieutenant Colonel Taylor and Major Reedy appeared in front of them, ordering them forward again. They climbed over the stone wall and surged across the strange field. A struggle to his left turned Richard forward. He shot the man straddling Matt.

Matt scrambled to his feet and ran forward without saying a word.

Huge rocks loomed ahead. Rallying cries erupted around him, and Richard opened his mouth, joining their battle yell. The relentless barrage of artillery continued. Richard reloaded his rifle, fired, and then surged forward, using his bayonet to ward off the enemy.

He barely noticed burns on the uniforms of the enemy and others near him, the close-range shots sparking the worn material of uniforms.

Shock bred rapid thoughts, but Richard focused on the hand-to-hand struggle with the boy in blue facing him. He continued to yell and then stood stock-still for a brief instant at the line of Federals in front of them.

As they moved between the rocks, bullets chipped pieces of the stone away, creating sharp projectiles. Richard shielded his face with his musket rifle. He kept moving.

A captain passed him. "A prisoner called this Devil's Den." He huffed the words and headed up the slope ahead. Big rocks lay everywhere.

Reason and reality blurred. Richard remembered Marc's words, "Keep moving." He did, along with the rest, with stops behind the boulders for cover and to commence shooting from the skirmish line. He caught a distant glimpse of friends from the Fourth and Fifth Texas moving up the hill they called Little Round Top. Those boys might bring them the victory.

Chapter Ten

Mrs. Johnson and Mrs. Wilkins sobbed in each other's arms. They ignored the handkerchiefs Jenny supplied. Her eyes met the distraught ones of Mrs. Cushman, who sat in a chair bedside her friends.

Mr. Cushman cleared his throat. "Ladies, if you will compose yourselves, I'd like to finish sharing this letter from Jenny's pa."

The petite Mrs. Wilkins sniffed and pulled away, grabbing the handkerchief from the wooden tray on the stool in front of her. Mrs. Johnson smoothed back her chestnut hair and followed suit.

Jenny cooled herself with her only folding fan. Why couldn't they talk on the porch? She guessed some conversations deserved privacy, but not one breeze had stirred the curtains by the open windows. Perspiration trickled under the bodice of her muslin dress. Her undergarments clung to her skin like damp rags.

Mr. Johnson held up a newspaper. "This news account of the actions at Gettysburg is astounding. So many of the commanders were injured, including Hood, Robertson, and our Colonel Manning, not to mention the leaders who died. We still haven't heard from many of our boys who survived." He hit the paper against his hand. "Please continue to read the letter, Alan."

"Besides the details about Marc and John, this letter from Jenny's pa did say young Sam from our town was injured. A bullet skimmed the top of his scalp. He could have died after lying on the field a while, but they retrieved him." Mr. Cushman glanced up at Jenny. "Your pa says the boy went by wagon with the rest of the hundred or more injured."

"Would you please remind me"—Mrs. Cushman's voice fell to a whisper—"of the ones he named as dead?"

Jenny's gaze took in the expectant faces around the room. Will frowned as if bracing himself. Jack kicked at the floor. Alice grabbed Dawn's hand. Florey drifted over toward her. Jenny put an arm around her waist.

Mr. Cushman shook his head. "The paper lists *some* names, but the letters coming in list others. We'll wait until we know for sure. What we do know is Marc and John have been taken prisoner. John was injured at the time, but we don't know how bad."

His wife stood. "And Richard?"

He gave her a gentle smile. "If you ladies had allowed me to proceed, you might know." Mr. Cushman held up the last page. "You'll observe there is another page included in this letter. It is written by our son."

Mrs. Cushman grabbed the last page of the letter from her husband's hand, skimmed it, and clasped it to her heart. Having been raised in a Virginia household of high standing, she could read and write at the level of her brother who'd attended a university. She'd helped her children and Jenny read beyond the offerings of their small school.

The other ladies rose from their seats and hugged her. Tears streamed down her face. "Oh, my dear friends, how selfish I feel."

Mrs. Johnson's gentle voice assuaged all the jumbled emotions filling the room. "Not at all, Ella. We are all blessed to know our boys are alive. Of course, Mary and I would prefer our boys to be with your son instead of with those Yankees, but our hope of a homecoming is not snuffed out today. Praise the Lord!"

Jenny longed to read the letter in private, but her father had not sent it to her. She lifted her gaze to find Mr. Cushman watching her.

"Jenny, your pa wrote more details of the battle I won't share with you." He retrieved the last page from Mrs. Cushman and handed the letter to Mr. Johnson. "He didn't want you ladies to picture the details."

She moistened her lips with her tongue, pressed them together, and swallowed hard. "The newspapers and those sketches—"

"—Allowed us more than expected, just as they did after Sharpsburg, or Antietam, as the Yankees call it. I understand there are stereograph cards featuring photographs taken there. I'm sure some of those photographers descended on Gettysburg after the battle. Personally, I don't want to see them. If we must, I prefer sketches to the visceral realities they're sure to show. I've seen battle in person. I've fallen on the field of battle. You ladies don't need to see it."

Mrs. Cushman stood. "Maybe we should. I don't mean being present at the battles, but some of the wives and mothers have visited their husbands and sons in camp. I've heard Mrs. Manning did. There are women nursing men in some of the cities and camps."

"Even some in private homes." Mr. Johnson folded the letter and placed it on the mantel. "Marc wrote me about that in his last letter." He removed his pipe from his pocket and lit it. "The men do love seeing the ladies when they visit, but it is rare. He stated he hoped none of you endeavored such." He cradled the pipe in one hand and took a puff. "They are grateful to the ones who help the wounded. But as far as you ladies are concerned, it's too hard of a trip and too difficult to say goodbye."

Mr. Cushman stroked his chin. "That's one reason none of our local boys have tried a furlough. A few from the other Arkansas companies have returned under orders, but those are over. Ever since the Federals took control of the Mississippi River, you know how hard things have become—supplies, mail, travel and more. With the fall of Vicksburg . . . " His lips compressed into a grim line, and his eyes took on that faraway look—the one appearing at daily intervals since his return from his service.

While waiting for him to continue, Jenny glanced over at Mr. Johnson, noting a speck of tobacco in his beard but refrained from comment. She sighed, relieved to see it fall unheeded to the floor when he took another puff.

Mr. Cushman continued to stare past them.

Jenny adjusted in her chair, and Mrs. Cushman wadded the front of her apron. All of a sudden, Mrs. Wilkins stood and dabbed at her face with the handkerchief. "I refuse to sit here any longer. Among the families sitting out the war in Rockport, we have neighbors who have lost their sons or husbands. We will do as we have throughout this fray; we will tend to them and not ourselves this day." She turned toward the other ladies. "I know my husband and Matt will be sending me a letter any day now. They will know more about John. In the meantime, would you care to join me in preparing food and checking on the others?"

Jenny eyed Will and Jack. She tightened her arm around Florey and whispered, "Do you think they'd let the boys take us fishing?"

Florey flashed a grin and stepped away from her. "Pa, could Will and Jack take Jenny, Alice, and me fishing? If we catch enough, we could cook the fish and share with our friends."

Mrs. Cushman actually smiled, blotting her face with the edge of her apron. "For once, I think that's a perfect idea. Supplies being short as they are, fresh fish would help us. We can prepare everything to go with it. The men can grab a couple of watermelons from the field garden—unless soldiers have snitched them again."

Mr. Johnson laughed. "We still have enough." He nudged Mr. Cushman. "Right, Alan?"

Mr. Cushman blinked and smiled. "I'm sure you're right."

Alice stayed close to Dawn. "I'm staying here."

Jenny gave her a compassionate smile. "I figured you would." Alice had not strayed far from home ever since the tree incident. In fact, she didn't like to go outside unless her pa or Mr. Johnson came with them.

Jack and Will remained sullen but followed Jenny and Florey out the door. As soon as they reached the bottom of the steps, Jack squatted and gathered a few small rocks and shoved them in his pockets. Will dashed under the tree and picked up a small broken branch.

Florey grabbed a stick.

Jenny laughed. "What are you doing? We're going to the fishing hole not the river."

"Pa says, 'you never know,' but he won't let me carry a gun," Will said.

Florey raised an eyebrow. "You still have your knives, don't you?"

Jack kicked the ground. "Nope, Pa's afraid the Yanks might take them from us, so he took them."

Jenny posted her hands on her hips. "And you think those rocks and sticks will defend us?"

Will's face remained stolid. "They'd create a distraction for you girls to get away."

Jenny shrugged. "You're almost a soldier's age, Will." She blotted away the sweat on her forehead with the back of her hand. "I trust you."

Will squared his stocky shoulders. "You should." He strode ahead of them, and Jack ran to catch up to him.

Florey let her stick drag in the dirt behind her. "How does our community recover?"

Jenny knew her young friend took things to heart. She'd need to help her talk it through. "We don't even know what the outcome of this war is going to be, Florey. None of us can answer that question."

Florey stopped walking and stomped her feet. "We just have to win."

"Until this last battle report, I didn't think we could lose."

"What's all this loss for then?" Florey's gray eyes, so like her brother's, filled with tears.

Jenny wondered the same thing, but she couldn't say so. When had death become so commonplace? So many of their friends had died. Without a funeral, she half expected to see them again this side of heaven, but—

"Jenny?" Florey's expectant face tilted up toward hers, awaiting an answer.

"The South tried to save itself." Jenny shut her eyes, regretting the words while uttering them.

"Don't say that! We haven't lost yet."

Jack called to them.

Florey took off running. Jenny shook her head and lifted her skirt hem, dashing to catch up with her.

They stopped by the Johnsons' farm and retrieved some cane poles. The boys dug some worms, and they headed for the fishing hole. Unlike most girls, Florey had been fishing with the boys ever since she could walk. Her sisters never enjoyed it.

Jenny wasn't fond of it but had gone with her pa. They each prepared their own poles and found a place on the bank. She swatted away a fly, wishing it wasn't so hot.

Florey shielded her eyes and gazed up at the blue sky. "I wonder what it's like."

Jenny finished threading her worm on the hook. "What?"

"To go up in one of those balloons?"

"Balloons?" What in the world was she talking about?

Florey dropped her hand and grinned. "Your parents didn't read you the news article about the hot-air balloon in Little Rock back in March of '60?"

Jenny shook her head. "Remember my ma couldn't read. Pa would have looked at that event as foolishness."

Florey giggled. "So did my pa, but Ma loved the idea and shared it with us. She even had us draw pictures of what we thought it must have looked like. Do you think they use those to spy in this war?"

Jack made a face and plopped down on the bank. "Somebody would shoot 'em from the sky."

Florey raised her eyebrow. "I think it's a fine idea."

Jenny would have never pondered such. "Hm, maybe."

"We can ask the boys when they come home," Will said, grabbing a worm.

"Sounds like a Yankee thing." Jack dropped his line in the water. "This is a good spot. Marc picked it. He'll come back and be proud of us."

Will plopped down beside his brother. "You're right. Our brother has never failed at anything. He may be a prisoner, but he'll get through it."

Florey moved from the bank to sit on a rock. "John is bigger and stronger than the lot of them, but Matt must be worried about him."

Jenny had a thought. "It seems Marc and John might be safer as prisoners than in battle."

Jack stood. "You think?"

Will grunted. "I don't know. Our aunt from Virginia wrote Ma about her brother. He's a prisoner of war and in terrible condition."

Jack bent over him. "He's not Marc."

Will shrugged. "No, he's not, but—"

"Nothing." Jenny could tell a fight was brewing. "We don't know anything. But we are fishing, right?"

Jack unclenched his fist and sat, picking up his fishing pole. "Right."

"I'll miss John's letters."

Had she heard Florey right? "What?"

Jack laughed. "John ain't written you."

Florey's cheeks went red. "Not directly, but he always put a specific note in his pa's letters or his own to let us know about Matt. Mrs. Wilkins shares them with me."

"Matt ain't written his ma?" Will frowned.

Florey shook her head. "Not many times."

"Hmph." Will pulled a fish to the bank. "He wrote me last month."

"Did not." Florey threw a pebble at him.

Will removed the fish, tossing him in the pail he'd brought. "I'll show it to you. His spelling is terrible."

Jack laughed. "So is yours."

Everyone grew silent for the next few minutes. Jenny responded to the tug on her line. "Ha! I got one."

Jack posted his pole on the side of the bank and removed the fish for her.

Florey started humming. Will shushed her, and she made a face. Jenny giggled. It felt good. She knew the boys and men who'd left for war loved to laugh and joke. Hopefully they hadn't lost that. Laughter made life worthwhile. Her smile faded, remembering their

community's lost soldiers. She prayed this war was
worthy of the cost.

Chapter Eleven

"Halt! Who goes there?"

Richard provided the countersign and commenced the process to relieve the sentinels with new men. "Post Number One, Arms Port."

The relief took their positions and commenced, "Shoulder Arms."

His guard-detail ranks filled in; those relieved fell in at the rear. Matt marched to the back. Richard didn't speak to him even though he could see the question in his young friend's eyes. Richard remained focused on his duty. "Support Arms. Forward March."

Upon the completion of rounds, his sergeant dismissed him for the evening, and Richard returned to his tent.

Matt stood outside it, waiting for him. "Did you write them yet?"

Richard had added a note to the letter of Jenny's pa, but—no, he hadn't written his family a detailed letter since before Gettysburg. Once his regiment moved from the place called Devil's Den to the height of Little Round Top, he'd thought they'd won, but how short-lived that proved to be.

Sure, they'd taken out the cannons, but they had to retreat when more Federals appeared to defend the high place. The sharpshooting they'd done from the cover of the huge boulders sheltering them in the wee hours still rang in his ears. The fall of night brought freedom from fire, but the moon refused to give enough light to find all their fallen comrades. Richard closed his eyes. The agony of the cries in the darkness still haunted him.

Richard and Matt had tried to find John, Marc, and Captain Richards but to no avail. One man said they'd all been captured after pulling John to safety. Another said, Marc and Captain Richards—Boyd—had returned to the fight after hiding John. When they'd gone back to find him after retreating from Little Round Top, they'd been captured. As the evening hours passed, news of other losses and injuries reached them.

Their dear Hood, Robertson, and Manning—all wounded but not dead. Thank the Lord. Later, Richard's thankfulness switched to grief in an instant when he heard of others they'd lost forever. The word of the deaths of some of his hometown friends hit Richard the hardest. His boyhood friend, Sam, had spent the night on the field wounded. They'd found him and carried him to one of the wagons. The doctors planned to send Sam away from the battle to recover.

Still, he felt the absence of Marc and John the most. It didn't matter how—

He cringed and ducked.

Matt bumped him. "It's just an owl."

"Shh."

Matt came to attention. "Yes, Corporal Cushman."

Richard grimaced, still hating his promotion. He noticed Matt had relieved himself of his rifle. "Is your musket in order?"

"It is."

Richard pinched the space between his eyebrows. "Well done." He heaved his breath. "Go get us a cup of whatever they're terming coffee and let me tend to my musket. We'll talk then."

Matt pivoted.

Richard ducked into his tent with his rifle, his mind moving to the morning of July the third.

The morning light had raised a curtain on even bloodier events. The Third Arkansas renewed their sharpshooting, remaining behind the rock-wall fortifications they'd added during the earlier sniper firefight. From there, they witnessed the failure of Pickett's charge, but also the victory of their own First Texans who'd joined the Alabamians in the defeat of a Federal cavalry charge in a valley below.

They still hadn't recovered from the loss of men and leaders. The next day, orders came to transport the wounded by wagon with plans to transfer the injured men to a train. Richard and the rest marched away from the bloodied fields. Torrential rains escorted them from Gettysburg on the afternoon and evening of July Fourth—more of a dirge than a celebration.

Richard stared at the musket in his hands. How many of these had been left loaded on the battlefield? Many had misfired or never had a chance to fire. He made quick work of cleaning it.

"Permission to enter." Matt's voice startled him.

"Granted."

Matt ducked inside with two steaming cups.

Richard stood and took one. "Sit down, Private—Matt." Richard took a sip. Not real coffee but warm. "We're off duty."

Notes of music from the band drifted on the night breeze. Richard shut his eyes for a moment, identifying the tune. He smiled and opened his eyes.

Matt sat on the small stump Richard used for a stool inside the tent. "You didn't answer my question. Have you written home yet?"

Richard squinted his eyes. "I added a few lines to the letter Jenny's pa wrote. They know I'm well. Have you?"

"No, and you know those lines aren't what I'm talking about."

"Why do you care?"

Matt stood. Richard couldn't get over how tall he'd grown since they'd left home.

"I wrote Will at the end of last month"—Matt's eyes flickered shut—"after our small skirmish with that cavalry at Manassas Gap near the passes of those mountains." His eyes opened. "I can't seem to write my ma."

"I like being south of the Rapidan again." Richard took another sip of coffee. "Has your father written her?"

Matt nodded. "Not until yesterday. He sent her those tintype photographs we had taken in Richmond. Those travel better than those ambrotypes, I'm told."

"Yeah, they don't break as easily, but I hope they survive the mail journey."

"Part of me does, and part of me doesn't. I'm changed, Richard. It showed in the picture."

"You've grown up, Matt. That would have happened here or back home."

Matt frowned. "That's not what I mean."

Richard wouldn't insult him by sidestepping the comment. "I know what you mean. Why do you think I'm having trouble writing? It's happened to all of us."

Matt's brown eyes held a haunted sadness. "Others manage in spite of it."

"It's because they're smarter than us. Writing home. Getting letters. Those are the things reminding us of who we were. I pray we get back to being those people soon."

"Do you think we can?"

Richard took another sip of the sweet-potato coffee. He reached in his haversack, retrieving the letter. "I received this today."

Matt took it. "Is it from your pa?"

"No, it's from my sisters. Each one wrote me a few lines. It'd do you good to read it. I need to reread it. They wrote it after they got the news about Gettysburg and received the only letter sent to them—the one Jenny's pa wrote. It took a bit for the mail to find us."

"They haven't received any others?"

"Not as of the day they wrote it."

"Do you think John or Marc have been able to send any letters from prison?"

"I'm not sure how that works but not this fast for sure."

"I wish I'd hear from John."

Richard lifted an eyebrow.

Matt clenched his fist and hit his knee. "He didn't die. I feel it. Besides, I've been praying for him." His voice softened, and he touched his chest. "I have this peace."

Should he tell him? "I've had trouble praying since Gettysburg and our last skirmish. Our long marches bringing us back to Richmond have given us all too much time to ponder things. I even talked to the chaplain. We're all looking for remedies, and there aren't any. It's war."

"How did it go from July to almost September so fast yet so slow?"

Richard grimaced. "It's war." He motioned to Matt's cup. "Drink up."

Matt took a sip and spit it out. They laughed. Richard emptied his cup on the ground and stood. He turned up the lantern.

"Take that letter to your tent. You'll like reading it, especially Florey's part."

Redness crept up Matt's neck. "I miss her."

Richard nodded. "I'm glad you appreciate her. Speaking of change—those girls will be young women when we get home."

"I know."

"Are your intentions still honorable?"

Matt straightened. "They are. If she'll have me."

Richard put his hand on his shoulder. "Read the letter. Let's plan on going home." He dropped his hand and straightened. "For now, you need to get to quarters."

Matt smiled before he shut the tent flap. "Good night."

A lump formed in Richard's throat, homesickness welling up for the first time in a while. "Good night, Matt." He missed John. Matt resembled him but had distinctive features all his own. He'd seen his influence on Bevil Henry. Hmpf. Sometimes it was like watching an impish devil and a saving angel with those two, but their unlikely friendship bonded them. If Marc . . . He still had the urge to talk to his friend at least a hundred times a day, but he couldn't. Would home be like that?

He pulled off his boots. Taps sounded in the distance. He blew out his lantern and adjusted his bedroll. What would Rockport be like without all the men they'd lost? He hoped those imprisoned came home. The exchange of prisoners had slowed, and most now looked at sitting out the rest of the war. Somedays he thought they had it better, but then he'd look at those they'd taken prisoner or talk to someone who'd been in a Federal prison camp. How were either better?

A stillness settled—the Comforter nudged his spirit. He prayed.

September brought new orders. He watched the faces of the remaining men in the Texas Brigade. Being ordered to separate from the Army of Northern Virginia to follow Longstreet into Tennessee received a mixed response. The thrill of being closer to home held possibilities of furlough for some, but many wouldn't even consider leaving their brothers-in-arms for a day.

The men certainly didn't want to leave General Hood behind. The original Texas regiments held firm to this belief, and the Third Arkansas shared their sentiments.

They moved back to camp around Richmond. Led by Colonel Manning during their night in the city, the men requested their beloved general come south with them. Richard breathed a sigh of relief along with the other men when the great man accepted the invitation.

They all celebrated, but once again Richard had to roll Bevil into his tent. This time, a sober and wiser Matt helped him. Private Henry and many others had a jarring morning train trip ahead. Richard and Matt wanted to enjoy it.

The next morning, it seemed all intended to enjoy the train ride—headaches and all. Even though they'd miss Virginia, the idea of heading to the more southern region had more than one soldier shouting and whistling. Richard puckered his lips, joining in on the favorite tune of "Dixie," and climbed on top of the boxcar. A Georgia brigade had boarded their train first. His beloved Texas Brigade boarded theirs next.

As a corporal, he'd managed to avoid riding inside the boarded box. He grinned, thinking about Law's Alabama men who'd follow them—a group of fine boys ready to see a bit of home.

As the trains passed towns along the route, women threw waves, smiles, and kisses their way. These proved not to be missed by the men inside the car beneath him. The fine Texans and Arkansans dismantled all but the roof and its supports. Bevil and Matt shinnied up to join him topside. A sergeant barked at the rest to stay below.

Richard laughed. Bevil winked at him, then almost fell off the train trying to catch the flowers a pretty young lady threw their way.

"Too bad she can't hear you." Richard folded his arms, grinning.

"I'll bet she hears this." Bevil put the thumb and forefinger of his right hand at the edge of his mouth and sent out a whistle so loud Richard grabbed his ears. It indeed carried over the rumble of the train. The young lady flashed a broad smile.

Similar pageantry from supportive villages greeted them. Richard couldn't help enjoying the stops the most. Bevil and other exuberant lads jumped from the train to take the gifts of food prepared by the towns' ladies. It seemed word had spread about their route heading west to Tennessee.

The rickety tracks needed work, but as long as they carried the train, Richard didn't care. It felt good to breathe without bullets flying around him.

By the time they reached Atlanta, Richard sent up a prayer of thanks. He sent up another one when they found Benning's Georgians had set up camp close to the tracks, waiting for them. Richard craved sleep, and the firm, non-moving ground felt good beneath his feet. According to their first lieutenant, they'd have a brief train ride early tomorrow, dropping them closer to the battle area.

Matt ran up to him, balanced on one leg, and held up his left foot. "I got a splinter from that railcar."

Richard steadied his friend. "I'm sure we'll receive our promised shoes before the next battle."

"Corporal Cushman, a word please."

Richard turned to find Jenny's father, now a third sergeant, waiting for him.

"Yes, Sergeant."

Matt promptly came to attention.

The sergeant's eyes flickered, and his shoulders slumped. "Private Wilkins, you may remain." The man's gaze held a sadness. "You both should know the news we must deliver to the rest of the Third Arkansas tonight. Little Rock has fallen to the Federals."

Richard couldn't breathe for a moment. Jenny . . . their families could . . . "Do you want me to help assemble the men?"

"Indeed, I do, Corporal." He smoothed his mustache and angled toward Matt. "Private, return to your company."

Matt pivoted and complied.

Little Rock. Only forty miles from Rockport. From home.

Anger sparked in Richard's gut.

Chapter Twelve

Jenny picked her way through the early autumn leaves, now half green and brown. She spotted the edge of a floppy hat and shirt sleeve peeking out from the opposite side of the tree trunk. *Just as she thought.* She approached the tree, reaching it in three paces. "Want any company?"

Florey didn't turn. "Not really, but I might need some." Her friend sat with her back against the trunk of the tree—her special tree. They'd always teased Florey about running to this spot to pout.

"Your pa sent me to fetch you home." Jenny sat down on the roots of the tree to the right front of her friend, so she could face her. Her friend continued to gaze at the pasture a little below the knoll of trees. "Florey?"

The stormy gray eyes blinked, softening like a dove. "I figured." Florence shifted, adjusting her pant-clad knees toward Jenny. "I'm in trouble for sneaking out, and once Pa sees me in these clothes, he'll have my hide."

"Then why did you wear them?"

Florence yanked off her floppy hat, sending her amber hair tumbling around her shoulders. "I had to get away from everyone. With the Arkansas newspapers run by Confederates closing and the mail service being about done, we aren't getting much news."

"The fall of Little Rock isolated the southern half of our state, but some of our boys are getting letters through by family members traveling home."

"Seems like they're not recruiting much anymore, and our boys were never ones to furlough."

Jenny grabbed a leaf and crumbled it, letting the crisp particles rain between her fingers. "We can't do anything about it. At least Mrs. Johnson received that one-page letter from Marc and John. It gave her and Mrs. Wilkins hope for their sons."

"Did it? They let me read it. Those Yanks had crossed out more words than they left for us to read. Why do they get to read the letters sent home?"

Jenny pulled up her knees under her dress and laid her head on them. "It's war, Florey. Both sides want to win. If they think the prisoners write anything they don't want Confederates to know, they blot it out."

Florey stood. "Guess I'd better go find Pa and the Johnsons. They're chopping wood today."

Jenny lifted her head, pushed to her knees, and then stood, balancing against the tree trunk. "I know. He said for you not to come this morning."

Florey twisted her hair and shoved it under her hat. "Guess I deserved that. What are we doing today?"

"Quilting."

Florey groaned.

"Just be glad we have those old clothes of yours and Alice's, the ones your ma and Dawn used to piece the squares. Mrs. O'Neal at the store in town has hidden all the fabric she had to keep the Yankees from stealing it. Your ma could have sat us at the loom today."

Florey huffed out a long breath. "Let's get to it. She's already insisted I knit Richard some more socks."

Oh, dear! "Poor Richard. You'd better leave those to me." Jenny linked her arm with her friend's. "Find your smile. Mrs. Wilkins and Mrs. Johnson are joining us, and I made us a treat."

A sideways glance caught the beginnings of a grin dancing on Florey's face. "It's sounding better, but we don't have enough to make those teacake treats Ma used to make."

"Salt and sugar are in short supply, but I did manage to make us little fruit pies. I'm sure glad they dug those wells close to Arkadelphia and used that evaporation process to get us more salt. As for fruit, our orchards supplied us well, even with soldiers snitching some."

Florence let go of her and whooped. "Race you!" She took off without another word.

Jenny knew better than to call her back, so she lifted her skirt, revealing her bare feet and took off running. She had to save her already worn-out shoes for colder weather. All of them knew not to expect any shoe shipments from the North. It felt good to run. Her chest burned, but she exulted in the unladylike exertion. Welcome joviality bubbled up, and she shouted with laughter. She bumped into Florey who'd come to an abrupt halt at the edge of the yard. "Caught ya."

Florey turned her head and placed a finger to her lips. She pointed. Jenny directed her gaze toward the steps of the porch.

A soldier sat eating something—*It had better not be her pies.* Jenny assessed his floppy hat and tattered butternut and gray clothes. Her heart twisted.

"He's one of ours."

Florey's shoulders relaxed, but she whispered, "Don't matter. Some of ours have turned mean."

Dawn appeared on the porch and handed a cup to the man.

Jenny bumped Florey and stepped around her. "Let's go."

As they approached, she noted the quilting frame stood undisturbed under the tree. A rifle lay within the soldier's reach.

Mrs. Johnson joined Dawn, holding another plate. She set it on the step above the one on which the soldier sat, positioning it to his left. Upon straightening, she glanced their way.

"There you girls are. Come and welcome Ephraim Johnson, my nephew."

Florey's gray eyes studied him, and then she gave an obligatory bob of courtesy.

Jenny had never learned to execute those genteel niceties. She bobbed her head instead. "Welcome, Mr. Johnson."

Florey kicked at the dirt. "I remember you. Your brother and you visited one summer when I was small."

The soldier resembled an older version of Marc, except he had blue eyes. He must be in his late twenties.

A broad smile appeared behind his dark brown beard. "You're right, little lady." He laughed. "That voice of yours gave you way."

Florence pulled off her hat.

Mrs. Cushman bustled through the door, carrying a set of men's clothes. "Florence Elizabeth, you come in this house and change clothes this instant. You'll also coil up your hair as fitting for a young lady."

Ephraim stood, and Florey extended her hand for him to help her up the steps—a deference her independent friend seldom made. Instead of offering his right hand, which was closest to Florey, he turned, extending his left hand. Florey glanced back at her with wide eyes, but then flashed Ephraim a bright smile and disappeared inside.

The unfilled right sleeve dangled at Ephraim's side. Tears welled up in her eyes. She turned away, swiping her face. He mustn't see her tears.

Mrs. Johnson hurried down the steps. "Please pardon us a moment, Ephraim." Taking Jenny by the arm, she guided her to the tree next to the quilting frame. "He arrived this morning after my Lee and the boys left. Ephraim has been discharged due to his limb loss. He made it home to Mount Ida only to find his wife, children, parents, and sisters had fled to Texas last week. Their nearest neighbor said the fall of Little Rock caused many heightened fears. From what he said, they're staying in a small community not far past the state line."

"Is he going to join them?"

"Of course, he will. It's just . . . he had a hard time getting home. Ephraim would like to stay with us at least a week before he heads for Texas." Mrs.

Johnson's blue-green eyes filled with tears. "He needs our men here to help him get stronger—to show him what he can still do instead of what he can't—before he goes. He's a good man."

"I don't remember him." Jenny glanced at the now empty steps. He must have gone inside to change into those clothes Mrs. Cushman had. She forced herself to attend to Mrs. Johnson's voice.

"As children grow, people get busy focusing on their own lives and communities—no matter how close or far away. He's nine years older than Marc. The last time he visited was that summer he and Dan, his younger brother, came. The year before you moved here. He married young and moved close to Little Rock with his wife. After the war started, she brought the children and planned to stay in Mt. Ida while Ephraim was away at war."

The image of a young man who'd visited the year they moved here flashed in her mind. "That explains it. Is his brother the lithe fellow who taught Marc about gentle-breaking of horses?"

Emily Johnson smiled. "Yes, so you do remember Dan?"

"I do. My mother liked him. She said he had some Indian ways about him."

"He should. His father's lineage includes Cherokee. The boys' mother is my Lee's oldest sister." Redness rose in Mrs. Johnson's cheeks. "Oh, dear, I don't want him to think we are pitying him." She took Jenny's arm again. "Let's rejoin him."

Jenny sat on the step below Ephraim Johnson, who had resumed his seat and meal. She noticed his uniform folded and stacked in one of the porch chairs. He sure looked more approachable wearing Richard's clothes. "Mrs. Johnson informed me of your relation. It seems my misfortune not to have met you in earlier times. My family—"

"You're the Jenny that Dan came home jabbering about after you moved here." He grinned. "Too bad his Matilda captivated his heart a couple of years later, or I'm sure he would have come calling soon."

"He's married?"

"No, but she is his intended with her father's blessing. I saw her yesterday. Her family is staying the course on their farm. Like all of you."

Florey joined them, plopping down in one of the chairs on the porch. Her calico dress had a smudge of soot on the front. "Jenny has an intended even though no one will say it plain."

Ephraim lifted an eyebrow.

Jenny wished Florey knew how to stay quiet. She put her palm to her cheek, feeling the heat rise. "I hope to have such a privilege with her brother Richard."

Ephraim took a bite of peas. "Lucky man. I remember meeting him. He's Arty's friend, isn't he?"

The thought of Arty brought a smile. She remembered when he helped them cut that tree off the road. "Yes, he is. I didn't know you knew him."

Mrs. Cushman pushed open the front door, pushing Alice ahead of her. "I need all of you to finish your gabbing and eating and clear this porch. Mr. Johnson needs to join the men. I'm sending Alice with him to show him the way. She has to stop hiding in this house."

"Ma—" Florey started, but the stern look Mrs. Cushman wore proved sufficient to stop any protests.

"The rest of us need to finish the quilt today. Colder weather will be here before we're ready. This war has left us little after all the raiding. I must make sure my family stays warm."

Jenny stood as Ephraim shoveled the rest of his food in his mouth.

He finished and stacked the two plates. "Thank you kindly, Mrs. Cushman."

Ella Cushman nodded and nudged Alice forward. "Get going. Will and Jack are there, so that should cheer you."

Ephraim picked up his rifle and gave Alice a gentle nod. "I'll keep you safe, Miss Alice. I was a good soldier. They even let me keep my musket."

A slight sparkle appeared in Alice's eyes. About time. A glow of contentment kindled in Jenny's stomach. War had taken away the gaiety of life. Only the returning soldiers could bring it back—*if* they returned.

Another voice blew courage into her spirit. *Your joy is based on much more.*

Chapter Thirteen

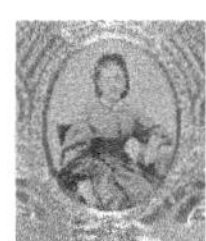

"Forward!" General Law ordered.

They topped a ridge and formed into a battle line close to a creek. Richard swallowed hard. Hoofbeats turned his head—General Hood! His arm might still be in a sling, but the men around Richard silently removed their hats in honor—the battle too close to whoop for him.

They followed the general, driving the Federals into the trees on the other side of the creek across a bridge. March. Double-quick. Keep moving.

Richard kept his shoulder in line with the men next to him. Another brigade of Confederates greeted them in the woods facing a road.

"McNair's Arkansas," the brigade called out, identifying themselves.

His heart lightened at the sight of them. Seeing other Confederate soldiers from their home state fanned the flame of purpose within him. He grinned. "This day feels better already."

Matt, marching next to him, allowed one word. "Yep."

Richard glanced sideways in time to see a broad smile grow on his friend's face.

In a bit, they passed a mounted cavalry from Texas. Their Texas boys greeted their fellow soldiers in kind.

They kept marching and moved into the usual alignment by company, with Law's Brigade on their right. They'd sleep in the same formation.

In the middle of the night, Richard stirred. Whispers to his right had him squinting in the gray night. Matt straddled Bevil from the First Texas, pinning him down. Were they going to fight? His young friend slid off Bevil before he could intervene.

"You didn't trick me. I knowed you weren't a Yank. Where'd you go?" Bevil whispered.

"The invisible outhouse."

Richard grinned and crawled over to them. "Hush, you two. Don't wake them Yanks before sunrise."

A restless night ensued. He tried to tune out the chopping sounds emanating from the Yankees beyond the trees. Instead, he listened for other sounds. The crackle of leaves, the snap of a twig, the croak of a frog, and the songs of the katydids and crickets. His mind vacillated from irritation to contentment and settled on the latter. The sounds of nature reminded him of home. If only an owl or bird could join the nighttime chorus. He wondered what the regimental musicians thought of the night music. Most of those creative souls wouldn't be fighting tomorrow—they'd help the doctors and the wounded. He turned his head at another sound.

Mr. Wilkins snored again, smacked his lips, and then flipped onto his side. Richard closed his eyes.

September 19, 1863

Something much louder than a snore woke him and the others at dawn. Artillery fire reverberated through the air. Richard jumped to his feet, rousing the few men still slumbering.

He listened, trying to orient himself to the direction of the sounds of battle, still distant enough to breathe . . . for now. This place had many thickets—an ample amount to disorient any division. How'd they know where to head without being able to determine the position of the enemy before they were right on them?

The men hurried to their feet. Some grabbed corn dodgers from their haversacks and prepared for the orders sure to come. Richard started to take a bite of his fare and almost put it away. Today it was as hard as Union hardtack. He'd almost broken a tooth on one before. They didn't have any form of coffee to dunk it in today.

The sound of a canteen being opened next to him made him pause. He glanced over as Matt poured a little water on his ration—Yank hardtack. He grinned. Matt must have held on to a cracker or two. They didn't dare use any of the rest of the rations they had cooked and stored in their haversacks. Most would save those for later. He shrugged and followed Matt's example, using a little water on his food. He took a bite. Still hard, but at least chewable.

The battle sounds intensified throughout the morning. At their sergeant's call, they organized the troops. Their captain told them to be ready by noon.

A rolling rumble sounded and the ground shook. Richard strained to see the sky hidden by the pine and oak trees surrounding them. Was a storm brewing? Murmurs echoed around him. Some of the men smoked pipes and relaxed while they waited.

Time passed, maybe an hour, and then the "Forward" order came.

The familiar mixture of excitement and fear churned in Richard's stomach. That mixture had fueled him in battle throughout the war. They marched ahead, stopping on command behind troops in gray ahead of them. He couldn't identify their company flag. His stomach calmed while they waited another few hours, but the sounds of the battle kept him ready at a slow churn.

By almost midafternoon, the bullets whizzed close enough to grab their attention. The orders came on their heels. They moved, following the voice of General Robertson at the head of the Fourth and Colonel Manning at their helm. Bullets erupted from the muskets of men on the ground, men behind trees, and every other place Richard couldn't see due to the trees and brush.

Under Law's temporary command of the three brigades of Hood's Division, they started the assault behind Gregg's Brigade with men from Tennessee and Texas and ahead of Benning's Brigade from Georgia.

Johnson's Division, with brigades led by Fulton, McNair, and Sheffield, moved forward to their right.

Good men from Tennessee, Arkansas, North Carolina, and Alabama filled their ranks.

Positions changed and adjusted. Johnson's Division moved ahead of theirs and spread out their brigades. Another Confederate division moved to their right, surging ahead, bolstering support. Richard recognized some of the Georgians.

He willed away the confusing changes within his peripheral vision. The blur of surrounding trees and glimpses of distant fields registered but didn't hold Richard's focus. His men surged ahead wielding their bayonets, trying to stay together through the brush and around tree trunks. Intense battle ensued at every juncture.

Richard loaded and fired without hesitating. Beside him, Matt did the same.

Ever since that moment when John fell injured at Gettysburg, Richard always adjusted his position to keep Matt in his sight. He'd promised John he'd keep Matt safe.

Ahead of them, another Confederate division he couldn't name broke apart. Their skirmish line engaged two Federal companies advancing on their left. The protection of the rest of Robertson's Texas Brigade fell to them—the Third Arkansas. Time passed unheeded. The battle in front of him consumed every muscle. The dance of battle continued. Forward. Fall back. A group of the Tennessee troops fell back, and the Third Arkansas surged forward. The battle movements had them fighting right and then left. Defending flanks. Attacking flanks. In the midst of the battle, Richard compared what he saw to a swarm of bushwhacking mosquitos swarming everywhere.

Richard reached and crossed a road. The troops swarmed into a field. A house and a barn in the distance came into view. Men started falling faster all around him. What kind of muskets were the Yanks using? He'd never heard such rapid volley fire. Finding their targets with pings and splats, the shots echoed in the air. The breath of death and a maiming hand advanced on them.

"Rich—Corporal Cushman!"

He turned. Jenny's father bent over another man. "Yes, Sergeant?"

With one last glance at Matt fighting a few steps ahead of him, he fell back to help. He grabbed one arm of the injured man, and his prospective father-in-law grabbed the other, pulling the man back. Richard stopped, thinking they'd gone far enough for the litter-bearers to find the soldier. Then he looked down—Carl Wilkins. Matt and John's father. He'd known him his entire life. The man moaned and tried to help them, but his legs gave way.

"Let's carry him to those trees, across from the creek where the brush-arbor tents are set up for the wounded."

They'd passed the tree line when some litter-bearers met them, dodging bullets.

"At this rate, we're going to have to leave many until nightfall, but we'll take this man from here."

They turned, heading back. Smoke stung Richard's eyes, and he had trouble seeing. He stopped, swiping at his eyes with his fingers and sleeve. Jenny's father dashed back onto the field ahead of him. Another man ran past him. Just then the man running the path he would have taken fell dead a few yards in front of him. Richard gripped his gun.

A moan and a plea came from a man belly-crawling toward him. How was the man moving? His head bowed low as if draped across a board on his stomach. Blood trailed on the ground after him.

Richard squatted. A bullet flew past, hitting the tree behind him. He touched the head of the man. A moan answered. Then another voice spoke. "He'll bleed out—I'm all that's keeping blood in him." He knew that voice.

"Bevil?"

Trepidation rattled his insides. He lifted the head of the moaning man. *Matt. No!*

Matt lay draped on Bevil's back.

"Bevil, we've got to get him off of you and bind his wound tight."

"Just a little farther."

Richard plopped on his stomach and crawled with them. He'd be little help to them if he were shot in the process, but they had to be quick. Richard gauged the distance to where the litter-bearers had been before. None in sight. He scrambled to his knees. "Stop here. I know where a medical tent is."

He pulled a threadbare shirt from his haversack and ripped it. Rolling Matt off of Bevil, he recoiled at the gut wound. His mouth went dry. Sheer determination moved his hands, and he wadded some of the strips and placed them in the hemorrhaging hole in Matt's stomach and then wrapped a securing strip of cloth around him.

Matt's eyelids flickered. Richard put his face near his. He'd passed out for now, but he was breathing.

Bevil rose to his knees.

Richard met his eyes. "Even though I'm not in your First Texas company, I'm the only officer of our brigade here with you right now. I am ordering you to stay with me. I'll accompany you back to the field once we move Matt to the dressing station. Ready?"

Bevil nodded and stood.

Richard scooped up Matt. They ran, almost fell, and ran again all the way to the area with a makeshift medical tent. He didn't know how they reached the place unscathed.

Bevil collapsed, leaning against the trunk of the closest tree. Blood ran off his back where Matt had been and pooled beneath him.

"You wait here," Richard said.

Amidst the other moaning soldiers, a doctor directed him where to lay Matt.

Richard stroked his friend's dark hair off his forehead. Still so young—just shy of his sixteenth birthday. Why had they let him come? Why had the commanders allowed him to stay? He knew many others who'd ignored the eighteen-year-old standard just as some of the older men had ignored their age cutoff. Clever ways around those limits abounded.

Matt's colt-like eyes fluttered open. Sweat beaded on his forehead. He licked his lips. "Richard, promise me . . . you'll be John's brother for me."

Richard blinked. "Matt, we don't—"

Matt's hand found his. "Promise me."

Richard nodded. "I promise."

Matt's weak grip remained steady. "Tell Ma and Pa I love them"—he swallowed, his Adam's apple bobbing—"Florey, tell Florey, I love her—and . . ."

Tears streamed from the corners of his eyes. "Make sure she marries someone who loves her."

Richard choked out, "Yes"—his own face covered with tears.

Matt squeezed his hand. "Tell Bevil to trust God."

The doctor reached them. Richard stepped back. The physician removed the bandaging and shook his head. Matt's eyes met Richard's as the man hurried away. Richard took his hand again.

"Say the Psalm."

Richard knew the one—the Twenty-third. He started, but Matt's gaze moved, lifting upward—the pain reflecting in them changed to peace, and then closed.

Everything in him wanted to scoop up his friend and carry his body back to Arkansas, but he couldn't. The doctor hurried back and then ordered two men to move Matt to the line of covered men already on the ground outside the tent. Richard asked about Mr. Wilkins and was told he'd heal. The time for telling him about Matt wasn't now, but he informed the doctor of the situation.

Richard found Bevil. The young Texan's eyes blinked and then narrowed.

"That bloody field and ditch, or was it a creek bed? The Georgians need— "

Richard hesitated then slapped him in order to refocus him. "Private Henry, we have more fighting to do."

Chapter Fourteen

Joy and sorrow arrived on the same day. The lingering brilliance of late summer colors mingled with the delayed but emerging autumn hues of the start of October in Arkansas. Life and death contrasted as summer and autumn did.

The postmistress pulled on the reins, stopping her wagon. A Saturday visit. Unusual. Mr. Cushman usually picked up their mail in town.

"Good morning, Mrs. Bailey." Jenny laid aside her mending, placing it on the stool in front of her chair on the porch.

Mrs. Bailey mounted the steps. "Is Mrs. Cushman at home?"

"You just missed her." Jenny stood. "She took Florey over to spend the day with Mrs. Wilkins."

Dawn approached from the direction of the barn, carrying a milk pail. "Good morning."

Mrs. Bailey bit her lip. "Where's Alice?"

Dawn inclined her head. Alice scurried up behind her with a basket of eggs. "Here I am."

"Girls, I have two letters here. One I have no idea of the contents. The second one I can guess. It's the reason I came here first."

Dawn's lips tightened. "How can you know what's in the second?"

"Because my granddaughter received one from her husband yesterday. He told about some of the deaths in a place called Chickamauga—in Georgia, close to Tennessee." She clutched the two letters to her bosom. "He named the boys they'd lost from our Company F."

Jenny gasped.

Mrs. Bailey reached her and gave her a hug. "No, my darling girl. He didn't name Richard or your father."

Jenny groped for the chair behind her and lowered herself. Her heart raced. Mrs. Bailey placed Jenny's sewing basket on the porch and sank onto the stool. "I am making a mess of this."

Dawn strode past them and into the house, followed by Alice. They reappeared in a few minutes without the milk and eggs. Food preservation meant self-preservation in these times. Alice ran out to the well and returned with a pail of water.

Dawn took it from her and disappeared again.

Alice leaned against the post nearest the steps. "Dawn poured the milk in that tin-milk jug and will set it in the washtub filled with our cold well water. It'll hold. She'll churn some of it later today."

An indulgent smile appeared on Mrs. Bailey's face. "You're a smart girl, Alice. Thank you for explaining it to us."

Dawn joined them, draping a shawl around her shoulders. "The wind has a little nip to it." She headed for the steps, but turned when no one else moved. "Are we going?"

Mrs. Bailey sighed and stood. "I never expected you'd all want to go, but I guess it's only right."

They trudged down the steps and climbed in the wagon. Jenny and Dawn shared the bench wagon seat with Mrs. Bailey, and Alice sat in the back. When silence ensued, Jenny's mind raced. Who were the letters from? She should have asked.

The graying wood of the farmhouse they approached mirrored the bleakness of Jenny's mood.

Mrs. Wilkins and Florey stood out front. Mrs. Cushman sat atop her wagon with the reins lifted, then lowered them and calmed the horse who whinnied and pawed at the ground, anticipating their departure.

Mrs. Cushman twisted around on her wagon seat. "Good morning, Mrs. Bailey. May I ask why you have brought my girls over here? I need them home doing their chores. I've allowed Florence to spend the day with Mrs. Wilkins."

The older woman held up one finger. "You'll understand."

Alice vacated the wagon, running to her mother's wagon. "Ma, you need to get down. She has letters and news."

Mrs. Wilkins tightened her arm around Florence's waist and stepped forward. "What on earth possessed you to deliver our mail in person, Vera Bailey?"

Mrs. Bailey climbed down from the wagon and extended the two letters. She tapped the top one. "I'd read this one first."

The brown eyes met those of the postmistress. "Why?"

Mrs. Bailey smiled. "From the Ft. Delaware mark on it, it might be from John."

Jenny nudged Dawn, and they climbed off the wagon.

Mary Wilkins took the top letter, leaving the other in Vera Bailey's hand. "It's the first letter written directly to me from John. Marc had mailed the first one to his parents and wrote in it of John's recovery from his wound. Please come into the house, my friends. I want to sit in my rocker to read this."

By the time all of them followed her inside and found seats around the table, Mrs. Wilkins was sitting in her rocker and had opened the letter. Unexpectedly, she read it to herself, but a small smile appeared. She looked up at them.

"It *is* from John and Marc. Both of them have written messages for us. I'll share this with Emily this afternoon. They've both been sick on and off, but say not to worry. Some of the rest of what he said has been marked out by the Federals."

Florey moved to sit in the chair next to Mrs. Wilkins, crossing her arms. "Mean Yankees."

Mrs. Wilkins patted her arm. "Paper is scarce, and getting mail out is an issue for them. I'm so thankful to have received this one page than to receive none at all." She twisted in her chair. "Thank you, Vera. My joy is complete today." She folded the letter.

Mrs. Bailey's hand shook as she extended the second letter. Florey rose and took it from her. "That's not Matt's print."

Mrs. Wilkins bowed her head. "Give it to me, child."

Florey complied and sank down next to her chair.

The crinkle of the paper removed the joy of the previous moment.

"It's from Carl." Mary Wilkins sniffed. "He was wounded at Chickamauga on the nineteenth of September, but he is recovering. The hot day of battle turned very cold that night, just like . . ."

Jenny held her breath, watching Mary Wilkins reading the next part in silence.

The small, dark-haired woman's shoulders began to shake. "Matt . . ." The letter fell from her hands. Tears streamed from her eyes.

Florey grabbed the letter. "No, no—"

Mrs. Cushman reached the rocking chair and grabbed Mary as she rose and her wail filled the room. She sank to the floor with her friend, holding her and rocking her.

Dawn turned to Alice and whispered, "Go ask Mrs. Johnson to come, and then go tell the men. They're repairing Mr. Johnson's fence."

Jenny understood loss. She'd lost her mother, but losing a child—

A tug on her sleeve turned her. Mrs. Bailey pointed to the door. Dawn rose, and they followed the postmistress outside. She'd lost two children to illness out of the six she had. This woman understood.

"I'll go let our neighbors who are still here know. Mary has tended to all the rest who have lost sons and husbands in this fray. Now it's our turn. I'm glad Carl is healing. We must pray the Good Lord allows him to come home to her."

Jenny ached. Why hadn't Richard or her father written? She turned to Dawn. "Chickamauga? That area is covered by the army of Tennessee. I thought ours were in Virginia. Why were they there?" Even though the newspapers no longer reached them, she'd read every one since the war started, studying the movements of all their men in gray.

Dawn's fair face paled even further. "I don't know."

The wind stirred and shook the limbs of the trees across the road. Yellow and brown leaves fluttered to the ground. Dawn tightened her grip on the shawl she wore. "Are any of them coming home?"

Startled, Jenny gasped.

Dawn's expression fell. "Oh, Jenny, I'm sorry. Surely the Lord will restore some of them to us."

Jenny stifled the impulse to run away. Her mind raced. Pa. Richard. Her eyes flew to Dawn—Richard's sister. "You're feeling the same things I am. Don't apologize."

Mrs. Wilkins mattered right now. Florey mattered. They'd lost Matt. She placed her hands on the porch rail. "Why Matt? I've never known a funnier, sweeter boy." She searched Dawn's ashen face.

Dawn sank down on the bench Mr. Wilkins had built. "He'd be the first to tell us to leave this to God. Remember when he was baptized in the river the same day as Florey?"

Their eyes met. *Florey.*

Dawn's eyes filled with tears. "My precious little sister."

A wagon raced into the yard. Mrs. Johnson jumped down and ran past them into the house. Florey ran out a few minutes later. Her swollen eyes and reddened face broke Jenny's resolve to stay strong. Dawn grabbed her little sister, wrapping her arms around her. Jenny came behind Florey, completing the circle of the comforting embrace. Neither she nor Dawn had any words. Death took lives and forever changed the lives of all left behind. Her friend's hopes and dreams had shattered today.

Jenny couldn't help thinking about all the families—of both the North and South. The hope of resuming the lives they had before the war faded. No matter the outcome, they'd never be the same.

Jack and Will came running into the yard, their eyes wild. "It ain't true," Will shouted. "Not Matt. I got another letter from him earlier this week."

Florey pushed away, disentangling herself. "Show it to me."

Jack stepped in front of Will. "He wrote it the night they got off the train. He told us they were headed for Chickamauga."

Dawn stepped off the porch. "Boys, he must have handed that off to someone to mail. I'm sure he didn't have it with him during the battle."

"You don't know that." Will hit Jack, knocking him to the ground. Jack's shocked face turned toward them.

Florey hurried forward, helping Jack to his feet. She stepped in front of Will. "Show me the letter."

His face fell. "It's at our house." He glanced at his brother. "I'm sorry. I just had to hit something."

Jack stroked his jaw and nodded.

Jenny wished she could hit something.

Chapter Fifteen

The entrance to December of 1863 blew bitter and frigid. Richard kept his head down, no longer shocked by the bloody prints his bare feet left on the icy terrain. Guarding these wagon trains had spiraled downward since the Third first received their detachment orders in mid-November. He pulled at his tattered coat. Plenty of time to ponder and pray, but he found himself doing more of the first. Too much had transpired.

On the heels of the events after their victory at Chickamauga, morale plummeted. Their division's spectacular engagement and the ultimate hard-won victory on the twentieth day of September had rallied them to keep going. The day had vacillated from victory to standstills from the start. Some even said their own soldiers had fired at them by mistake. How could anyone know for sure?

Richard never stopped to analyze the origin of the shots, as long as he avoided them. They moved forward. Orders called for retreat and then forward again.

Every plunge of his bayonet had been for Matt, but God found a way to remind him of the futility of revenge. He peered into the eyes of a boy not much older than his friend, then pulled his bayonet from his enemy's gut, almost dropping to his knees. One thing kept him moving—Home.

Most said the last battle—fought on Snodgrass Hill, or some called it Horseshoe Ridge— set the boys in blue on the trail of retreat. The overall loss of Confederate men and officers at Chickamauga provided a bitter aftertaste in Richard's mouth.

Once again, their dear Colonel Manning received an injury. The doctors said he'd recover from the mild damage, but for what purpose? Too many had fallen, including their cherished General Hood, losing a leg as a result. They'd lost Major Reedy forever . . . and Matt.

Richard believed it was General Bragg who had forfeited their ability to win the campaign of Chickamauga and Tennessee. His inaction on the last day of Chickamauga became a pattern continued throughout October. The other generals churned and steamed like locomotives chained to the track. President Davis even came to meet with Longstreet and the others.

The image of listing ships without sails or a captain to guide the fleet came to Richard's mind. Law, a senior brigade commander, who'd taken temporary command of Hood's Division, faced replacement by Brigadier General Jenkins. Richard admired General

Law. He and many of the men chewed hard on the news. The shaken leadership impacted all of them as they followed and then awaited more orders near Lookout Mountain.

In late October during a nighttime skirmish at Wauhatchie—they preferred to call it the Battle of Raccoon Mountain—the Fourth Texas and a regiment from Alabama followed orders that Jenkins had initiated, and Longstreet approved—to their folly. As the rest of their brigade had other duties, Richard could never recount the events, but he sure laughed when the members of the Fourth retold them.

It seemed they'd marched up the mountain ridges only to have the shadows below them light up with the fire from unseen Yanks. Retreat—what a demoralizing end for them in one way, but after the fact, it became a matter of legend and laughter. They'd descended so fast they couldn't find a way to stop, until the trees, branches, and the bodies of their free-falling comrades lent them assistance. He knew the story told by the Fourth Texas would be retold many times.

Of course, the commanders found no mirth in the lifesaving turnabout of the troops. Instead, the failing commanders had to place blame on others, but this time they went too far. General Robertson endured a board inquisition and reprimand. *How dare Bragg blame others*? The other men had expressed it with a bit more color. Richard spat on the ground at the memory.

He'd hoped to get a furlough when small whispers circulated of the possibility. His heart ached for home. Matt's father had told him of his hard-written letter. A response from Mrs. Wilkins had yet to find him. The few furloughs offered dwindled to nil. It was just as well—how could anyone come back at this point? One of their ever-faithful men had never returned from a recruiting furlough. Richard planned to pursue an explanation from the otherwise steadfast officer if he made it home.

As for himself, he could never leave his brave brothers-in-arms. Unless God deemed otherwise, he'd stay to the end.

Longstreet moved toward smaller skirmishes during the Knoxville campaign. Marches carried them to more picket duty and then to the guarding of wagon trains. The Texans rejoined them a little past mid-November. It bolstered his spirits to see Bevil and the rest, but nothing improved their circumstances.

The aching tentacles of hunger and lack, accompanied by the icy fingers of winter, tightened as news of the general named Grant circulated. He'd taken over the helm of the Union's movements in Tennessee and herded Bragg and his men back to Georgia. Part of him had to smile at someone thwarting Bragg, but not at the expense of his fine men.

Richard didn't like being irritated, but it seemed the actions of the higher command did nothing but annoy him of late. Not only General Bragg, but also General Longstreet—too many leaders sought to control the chess pieces and the right to choose and replace their fellow-commanders.

In his mind, it did little to strengthen them and decreased what unified them. His pa had taught him loyalty. When the opposite seeped into the ranks, it weakened the confidence of the soldiers. Would they still give General Hood a command after he healed from losing his leg? The general had too much knowledge and skill . . . no, they'd utilize him in some capacity. Richard hoped he'd see him again.

"Halt!" The order came from the front.

They stopped for the night. Once settled, Bevil appeared by his tent.

"I have something for ya."

Richard saw the hides in the Texan's hands. He looked down at Bevil's feet. Such hides encased them. "Sam gave them to me. He wore some today. Said they won't last but will help for a bit. Just remove them before warming your feet near the fire."

Richard chuckled. "I'm not dumb enough to set my feet ablaze."

Bevil scowled. "Naw—it dries out the hides and makes 'em too hard to walk in with any comfort."

"Oh, well, thank you. For tonight, I'm warming my bare toes slow by the fire. They'll defrost or fall off— I'm hoping for the first."

Bevil grinned. "I did some praying today. It may not be soon, but things will improve."

Richard adjusted his cap. "Maybe I need to start praying. I've been rehashing everything all day."

"Matt's right"—Bevil swiped his nose and blew his breath into his cupped hands—"prayer makes all the difference. Instead of thinking on the losses and mess, I've prayed for the families of each of the fallen men today, especially the ones I knew."

Richard ducked inside his tent just enough to place the hides on the thin blanket—the one Captain Richards had given him that night outside of Richmond. It had served him well but needed replacing—just like every stitch of clothes hanging from their Confederate ranks. The oil cloth beneath the blanket provided his only protection from the moisture and ice on the ground. He sighed. "I think I'd better start praying as well, Private Henry. I'm plumb disgruntled."

"Matt used to say you choose what you think on. The chaplain gave me one of those little testaments. You know I got him to baptize me in that creek at Chickamauga the day Matt died—well, that night."

"Really? It turned cold that night."

"It felt invigorating to me."

"That's more than the water. I remember when I got dunked after a Sunday service back home."

"Yeah, while I sat beside that tree waiting for you to bring me news about Matt, I prayed for salvation. Do you realize God picked us to survive?"

This startled Richard. "What do you mean?"

Bevil eyed the fire a few feet from them. "Let's go over there."

They settled around it with a few of the other boys. Most sat staring into the flickering flames, too cold to talk but not Bevil.

"The sergeant called on you to help him pull a man off the field. Neither of you got wounded. Then, I crawled with Matt on my back, reached you without injury, and kept you off the field. I watched the man fall who sidestepped you and took the field. He died."

Richard stared at the sparks when the top piece of wood burned down, shifting into the embers. "I hadn't thought about that, but that last part gave me pause before we took Matt to the dressing station. Also, we made it there and back to the field. Why us?"

Bevil smiled. "I don't have to figure out that one. It's in God's hands, but each day has something for us.

Tomorrow might not. I'm not thinking past each day anymore."

The two other men who sat around the campfire with them looked at each other. One stood. "You talk too much. I think I liked you better before with all your pranks." He walked away.

The other held his hands over the fire for a moment before glancing up at them. "I needed that." He tipped his hat and disappeared into the darkness.

Richard stood. "So did I, Bevil." Matt's face danced in his memory. He even recalled him as a baby. "If he could see us, Matt would be pleased with you."

Bevil grabbed a couple of sticks and added them to the fire. "Don't think he has to worry about us no more, but I might ask him when it's my time. G'Night, Corporal."

Richard retreated to his cold blanket. Maybe that's how soldiers made it home—by not wrestling over the destination—Rockport or Heaven. He'd leave it to the Lord. *Just keep fighting.*

Mid-December brought more command chaos with accusations and charges. A man's word didn't seem to be worth much. By the time Christmas arrived, Richard's stomach had merged with his backbone— hunger gnawed it away. The reality of the dwindled number of men from Rockport set those remaining into action when rations never came. They knew how to hunt and forage. To the dismay of the Yank-supporting farmers in the area, Richard's fellow soldiers lifted a few sheep for their company alone, the pangs of hunger overpowering the pangs of guilt.

Thankful for a full stomach, Richard could only repent for not sharing it outside their company. Even though they buried the evidence, word of their escapade spread but no immediate reprimands or comments followed. The continued lack of supplies pushed other companies in the brigade to enlist the skills of his hometown friends. Richard grinned. "You have official orders to forage food from every Yankee-friendly farm in the area. Take enough to feed our brigade."

Another change in division command came about the same time. Richard didn't know Major General Charles W. Field, but word of his reputation circulated. That didn't bother him as much as the replacement of General Robertson.

"Did ya ever hear of this Brigadier General John Gregg?" Richard asked Jenny's father.

"He was wounded at Chickamauga and also fought at Vicksburg. Think he's a lawyer and judge by trade."

Bevil cleared his throat. "He's a Texas man. Born in Alabama, but he has lived in my state for a long time." He rocked back on his heels. "He'll never be Robertson, but he'll do."

Richard couldn't move past General Robertson's departure just yet. "We'll see. What I want to know is when are we going back to Virginia?"

The sergeant lifted an eyebrow. "When we receive orders."

A slight smile broadened the grin on Bevil's face.

Richard laughed. "Indeed."

Those orders did not come until April. Climbing aboard a train had never felt better. Nothing could beat the relief he felt, or so he thought. He grabbed his gear.

By late April, they disembarked at Charlottesville to a wonderful surprise—new clothes and shoes. He, along with the other men, jerked off the thin tatters posing as clothes, hoping the crawling pests might depart with them. Richard predicted he'd sleep well that night. He didn't. Nightmares woke him. He prayed until reveille. This pattern continued over the next weeks.

Once they received the "Forward" command in May, his zeal for their cause revived, and he enjoyed the jokes and pranks of the privates. The frequent questions from the ranks regarding their destination started. Richard answered when he could, but only with vague references to the general direction.

When they stopped to bivouac, then he gave the specifics, either revealed by passing through a town, or by information from the other officers. Stops at Gordonsville, then camping near Brock's Bridge and— he smiled at the next one—their stop to bivouac at Richard's Shop followed. Word circulated of fighting nearby. General Gregg followed the orders of their new division commander, Major General Field, who consulted with General Lee and General Longstreet.

When the artillery sounded in the distance, they marched into the wee hours toward a specified destination—Plank Road. They found a congested path of other soldiers, horses, and wagons on the road. Without halting, they pushed forward.

Events blurred. Richard's heart raced; adrenaline pumped. They moved left and north of the road. Their brigade line reformed. They moved up a hill and then down. Richard glimpsed Jenny's father and Sam adjusting within the line.

General Lee cheered them forward. *God bless him!* Richard respected their new brigade commander, General John Gregg, when he reminded them of Lee's presence in their midst.

The general couldn't mean to surge forward with them. Richard's voice joined others from their ranks begging the general to return to a position of safety. Once others encouraged the same, Lee moved away from their battle line.

Richard threw back his head and let out the Rebel yell. A crescendo of responding yells from the surging troops joined his. Where were they? Did it matter? He fought with everything in him. The frenzy of the fray had a rhythm beyond the drums.

He loaded his weapon faster than ever, fired, and reloaded. The taste of the powder when he tore the cartridge pouch quickened his loading. He pushed the bullet in place, whisking the ramrod in, out, and returned it to position. Brush, scrub oaks, and briars reminded him of his previous battles, but somehow this well-named place was unique enough to remain lodged in his memory—The Wilderness.

He listened for Colonel Manning's voice but never stopped advancing. There was no time to identify those bearing the colors or the shifting companies of the foe. Sweat drenched his hair under his cap, then trickled down his neck and into his eyes, making everything blur. He swiped it away with his fisted hand, still gripping his weapon.

Colonel Manning fell but was moving.

Smoke billowed. The stench of gunpowder filled his nostrils. A bullet pierced him—knocking his left shoulder back. He staggered backwards a few feet, but shock numbed him, and anger—or was it righteous determination that spurred him forward? Defense of his friends, commanders, and love for his family at home flowed through him. He'd do his best, follow those in charge of him, and let God decide the rest.

By nightfall, the woods burned. Richard dug trenches with those beside him, trying to escape the fire and heat. Screams came from the inferno. Richard heaved a breath and rested for the first time, just long enough to take stock of their losses. Brigadier General John Gregg had received severe wounds. Richard called for his sergeant, Jenny's father—killed. The pattern repeated for many officers.

Bevil ran up to him unscathed as Richard stood in the trench. "You're wounded." He returned with a soldier who could render him medical attention.

"General Jenkins died, and General Longstreet also got it in the shoulder plus in his neck, but he's in much worse shape than you are." Bevil knelt down. "One of our own got them by mistake today. They say it might have been the same shot that killed Jenkins."

Richard winced as the litter-bearer tended him.

"The bullet went out the other side, but we're getting you out of here. You won't fight tomorrow." The man signaled the other litter-bearer.

Richard shook his head. "I'd rather stay."

"These fires are out of control. Your shoulder will render you a detriment. I need to tend your wound better. You don't want infection to set in."

Sam, the youth closest to Matt's age from home, hobbled over to him. "Go with him, Richard. I lay out on the field at Gettysburg almost too long. That won't happen this time. I recovered, but it took months for me to get back to all of you. We need you, Corporal Cushman."

Sam's bloody foot caught his attention. That boy—like so many—kept going. He must have a purpose.

Bevil leaned forward and whispered, "Do it for Matt."

Richard nodded but held up his hand. "I'll go with you, but I can walk on my own." He grabbed his gun and nodded in the direction of two men hurrying toward them with a stretcher. "Looks to me like Sam might need those litter-bearers though."

Two of their regiment's band members—today litter-bearers—hurried up, and Sam acquiesced.

They shared a grin. Bevil sent them off with a weary salute.

Richard glanced back at the blazing trees, steeling his heart against the screams of agony filling the night.

Vacillating between the pain screaming in his shoulder and the grief in his heart, he followed them in ever-alert wariness away from the fires and into the darkness. This time *he* would have to write the letter home, but not until this fiery battle reached its final resolution. Maybe by then he could find adequate words to express his sorrow, and his father could convey them to Jenny for him.

Chapter Sixteen

Jenny ran, not caring if bushwhackers, guerrillas, or soldiers caught her. The horrible words telling of her father's death replayed in her mind. Why had it taken a month for Richard's letter to reach them? Her side ached by the time she reached the cabin. Her family's cabin. *Family.* Her parents had buried two babies before they had her. No others followed. She'd known a few orphans.

She'd also read about orphans in a three-volume book set Mrs. Cushman had shared with her— *Oliver Twist; or the Parish Boy's Progress* by Boz—more often known as Charles Dickens. A Virginia cousin, upon his return from England, had sent the set the year before the war started.

The volumes moved in migratory fashion between readers, passing from Mrs. Cushman, to Dawn, and then to her after Florence disdained it as too dreary.

She'd loved his writing. That's why Mrs. Bailey had loaned her the *Harper's Weekly* copies when they featured chapters from one of his other novels.

The terrible conditions described horrified her, but the characters touched her heart. She laughed, cried, and got angry. The beautiful words held sway over the lure of the hour of rest Mrs. Cushman favored for her girls on scorching summer afternoons or freezing ones. Now, her swollen eyes surveyed the inside of the abandoned cabin, searching for signs of life from her family.

She sank to the floor into the nothingness surrounding her. *Orphan.* She'd thought the loss of her mother had helped her understand Oliver, but today she felt *with* him—no, not exactly. At least she had known her mother and father. She'd had a distinct advantage over one born in a workhouse. *What am I thinking*? Her mind and heart raced.

She collapsed in a pile face down, her forehead resting on her forearm. Oliver wasn't real. She whispered, "I'm the real orphan. God, help all of us the war has orphaned." Dark words hinted someone else had orphaned her. "No!" She screamed, pounding her fist on the dusty floor. She lifted her head and lowered her voice. "God didn't do this! Man did."

The door burst open behind her. Panic squeezed her throat. She scrambled toward a corner.

"Jenny, Jenny, it's only us." Mrs. Cushman's arms surrounded her. Jenny clung to her, resting her cheek on her shoulder.

Mr. Cushman stood in the doorway. "Let's get her home, Ella. I'm sure others heard her. " He hobbled forward and scooped her up in his arms.

She couldn't let him do that—his knee. "I can walk."

His lips compressed, and he continued out the door and to the wagon, depositing her in the back of it. Jenny grabbed the wooden side and scooted against it, pulling her knees up under her non-petticoated dress.

"I want to ride in the back," Mrs. Cushman said.

Mr. Cushman's eyebrow lifted. "Your mother would be dismayed."

"That was another life, dear husband."

He assisted his wife onto the edge of the wagon bed. In a delicate move of Southern lady-like synchrony, she somehow scooted backwards with her worn-out petticoats in place and gathered Jenny against her side by the time her husband had climbed onto the wagon seat.

He glanced back at them. "Ready?"

Mrs. Cushman gave him a brief nod. "Yes." She grabbed the side of the wagon with one hand, keeping her other arm around Jenny. The horse pulled the wagon along the bumpy, undulating road.

Jenny hadn't been to the cabin in months. After Major-General Frederick Steele's Yankee men had stormed through at the end of March, building a pontoon bridge across the Ouachita River at Rockport, even Florey had stayed home. The construction on the courthouse had ceased, and the officials sent the records to Texas to save them from the Yanks. The soldiers' actions had destroyed homes and deprived them of food.

The hungry soldiers took anything they wanted. The Yanks stole some hogs from them and livestock from other farms. It could have been worse. For some of their neighbors, it was. Jenny recalled the Yankees who came by their farm. They'd demonstrated some social graces and acted polite upon seeing them.

One Union private smiled and declared they were the prettiest sights he'd seen in months. He even offered to pay Mr. Cushman a modest sum for the hogs. At least they'd arrived before their spring and summer crops had sprouted, sparking hope for the late spring and early summer.

The skirmishes and marches had increased. A soldier had shot the doctor's boy. Mr. Cushman declared the town a hollow shell in the wake of all the citizens who'd left. He and Mr. Johnson watched over Mrs. Wilkins and no longer allowed the women to go to town. Loss . . . loss . . . did one ever get used to it?

She stared up at the blue June sky. Everything in nature shouted life, in contrast to the delayed news of her father's death she'd received that morning. The sun burned bright, and she hoped rain interrupted it soon. They didn't need a summer of drought.

Wait. She hadn't even asked about the rest of the letter. Mr. Cushman always read the letters to himself before sharing them. She knew he sought to protect them, but he'd sent for her late in the morning without the other girls or Mrs. Cushman.

After hearing his simple words—"Jenny, I am so sorry, but your father has fallen on the battlefield. He is with our Lord"—she'd ask to see the letter.

Written in Richard's sloping handwriting, the first paragraph read, *"I don't know how to write this. As you know, the angel of death hands out thousands of calling cards on the field of battle. Some refuse to receive them and somehow survive with or without medical care.*

Others succumb and welcome him or God intervenes and sends his angels of light to bring them home beyond us. Please take care in sharing the news I must impart—Jenny's father has died in the midst of the Battle of the Wilderness. I—"

Her hands had gone limp, and the pages fell from her hands, leaving the rest unread. She'd run to her room and stayed there, refusing the midday meal. By midafternoon, following bouts of tears, the walls had seemed to compress and imprison her.

She turned her head. "What else did Richard's letter say?"

Mr. Cushman didn't turn in his seat but responded. "Ella, tell her what I shared with you."

Mrs. Cushman stroked her forehead. "Richard was wounded—"

"No!" Jenny sat straight up, her heart racing. "But he wrote the letter."

"He is fine, dear. The bullet passed through his shoulder. They tended him. He went on to fight at another place called Spotsylvania and then Cold Harbor." Her eyes looked toward her husband. "More terrible fights—Richard said so, did he not?"

Mr. Cushman still didn't turn. "Indeed. The boy has been too busy to worry about sending us a letter, but he did. He also mentioned receiving word of the death of Major General J. E. B. Stuart at a battle away from them—a battle at—"

"Didn't he include a few lines just for Jenny?"

"He did. I'll share them if she'd like to read them."

Tenderness trembled inside of Jenny. "Yes, sir. I believe they will bring me comfort."

Mrs. Cushman hugged her, and once Jenny relaxed in her arms, she smoothed her loosened hair away from her face. "We want you to know something, Jenny."

Jenny tilted her chin up, searching the kind blue eyes gazing at her. "Yes, ma'am?"

"In our eyes, you are our daughter from this moment forward. Even"—her voice broke—"if Richard doesn't return to us."

The enormity of everything filled her. She flung her arms around this well-mannered, at times stern, but compassionate woman and sobbed. "I love you."

Mr. Cushman reined the horse, and they tumbled into a heap. *Oh, dear*! Jenny lifted her head. "I'm so sorry."

Unexpected laughter burst forth. She had never heard Mrs. Cushman laugh like this. She disentangled her limbs and assisted the dear lady, joining in her laughter.

The girls poured out of the house but pulled up short as Mr. Cushman helped them from the wagon, chuckling all the while. Dawn's expression changed from concern to mirth. Florey and Alice smiled.

Mr. Cushman posted his hands on his hips and then waved them forward. "Don't just stand there gawking. Help your mother and Jenny into the house while I tend the horse and wagon."

The girls clambered down the steps, but Mrs. Cushman composed herself and held up her hand. She smoothed her skirt and bodice. "Grief is an unusual emotion, girls. We must allow ourselves the highs of it to dispose of the lows." Still taller than Jenny, she leaned down and kissed her forehead. "I'll see to supper."

"It's ready—sparse though it may be," Dawn said.

Mrs. Cushman patted her arm. "Thank you for allowing me a breath. I believe I'll sit on the porch and wait on your father. You girls go on inside."

Florey linked her arm with Jenny's. "We made something for you." They hurried up the steps. Once inside, Florey grabbed the sewing basket.

She cupped her hands over her mouth and nose. This must be a joke. Florence hated sewing. "Florey—"

"It's from all of us," Alice said, smiling with a moist brightness in her eyes.

Jenny dropped her hands, rubbing the palms against her skirt. "What have you done?"

Dawn unfolded the top item from the basket. "It's a family flag. We haven't finished it yet, but it's started. When the boys marched away, the ladies presented them with a company flag. We decided our family deserves one for serving on the home front together. The background is from the worn shirt Pa wore home from the war. We took strips of cloth from the worn ones in the mending pile. Most were beyond repair, but they came from each of us. Then we shaped them into a cross instead of crossed bars. All that's missing are the stars for the members who have fought, died, or are still fighting. We thought you could make those."

Tears filled Jenny's eyes. "I'd like to put a border on it for my ma. She kept some ribbon in her basket. I still have it."

"That's a fine idea." Dawn handed her an old shirt of Richard's. "You can cut the stars from this."

Jenny hesitated. "Do we need different colors for each?"

Florey bit her lip. "Why don't you do one for our pa with the scraps left from us cutting the base. He made it home. You choose what to use for your father, and then we'll see about Richard."

Her eyes filled. "This is thoughtful. My heart needed this. Should we hang it up somewhere?"

Dawn's eyes sparkled. "I'll ask." She ran out the door.

Jenny could hear her talking with Mrs. Cushman. She returned, smiling.

"Ma says we will place it above the mantel."

Jenny clapped her hands. "It'll remind us to stay unified and hopeful every day." She scanned the pleased faces surrounding her—sisters in Christ and family by adoption this day. A peace filled her. She gasped when a soul-deep hug squeezed her spirit. How could she explain it? She couldn't, but in that moment, she understood the comfort from the Comforter.

She would cry for her father tonight. The hope of his coming home to her had ended, but he'd gone to be with the Lord, and her mother must rejoice in seeing him. Even the siblings she'd never known must have greeted him. She'd trust Heaven with the details.

God had placed her in the Cushman family—with or without Richard's return. *Lord, I want him to come home. Thank you for all the Cushmans. I am so loved. You have done this. Please hug my pa for me and keep Richard safe.* She sighed and sat in the small sewing rocker beside the fireplace. "Time for the first star."

Florey handed her the flag and cloth scraps. "The Cushman family flag."

The front door opened. Mr. and Mrs. Cushman entered arm in arm. Seeing them, they stopped.

Mrs. Cushman smiled. "I'm glad you like the girls' idea. Why don't you finish it after supper?"

Mr. Cushman walked to the mantel. "Will you trade your sewing for a few words from my son?"

Jenny smiled, putting the flag aside.

He riffled through the pages and handed her the last one. "Here you go. He managed to procure a page just for you. Hope it says enough."

Taking the page from him, her hands trembled. She took a deep breath, inhaling the aroma of cooked chicken and cornbread. Knowing she had to hurry but wanting to linger over the words, she read:

Dearest Jenny (Please don't find me too forward for this endearment),

War has taught me not to leave things unsaid. Forgive me, for I have left many things unspoken with you. Yes, an understanding has lingered between us, but the time for the utterance of it seemed ill-conceived. It is my desire to look into your beautiful brown eyes and speak the words in my heart.

If this war doesn't allow me to return to do so, we must leave this in the hands of the Almighty. But if I return, my intent is to ask for your hand. Your father knew this, and I felt we had his blessing in his interactions with me. It was a privilege to serve first alongside and then later under him. He handled the duties of a sergeant with dignity and honor. I always respected him before he joined us in the war, but my esteem grew. He is missed in our ranks along with so many others.

My grief for you in this time of sorrow is immense.

I have no right to assume your affections haven't changed in my absence. This war has moved us from boys and girls to men and women. Unless you write me otherwise—and I do hope Ma and Pa will allow you to correspond at least this once—I will hold to the hope of a happy reunion at the resolution of this conflict in which our men have shown themselves faithful and mighty.

Read my heart in my closing.

Ever yours,

Richard

Mrs. Cushman called from the back of the house, "It's suppertime, Jenny."

"Yes, ma'am."

Jenny read the last three words again, *Ever yours, Richard,* She exhaled, giddy yet at peace. Again, she scanned the letter. Richard's penmanship sloped in smooth lines for most of the page, but a few of the letters appeared shaky. She bowed her head and whispered a prayer. *"Lord, please strengthen Richard. If he's sick, make him well. Please bring him home— Amen."*

"Jenny?"

"Coming."

She folded the cherished page and dashed to place it inside the sturdy cover of the beautiful volume of Dickens on the small table at her bedside.

Chapter Seventeen

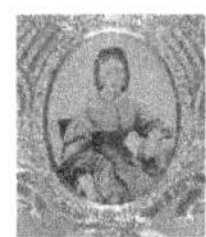

Richard found himself promoted to sergeant during the long, hot month in the trenches of Petersburg.

"Heads down! Move away." The Federals sent more trench mortars their way. They ducked at the sound, and then looked up, gauging where it might land, then dashed to the opposite side of the ditch. "Bomb—left!"

After the loss of so many friends, along with the ever-present pangs of hunger and possibility of death, a strange inner stillness settled on Richard. Since the beginning of the war he'd existed on the reality of nightmares rather than romantic dreams. Few to no letters had reached them. Home became a far-off country within a nation divided.

War—how could they go on living after it? He prayed God might grant him the opportunity, but contrary to the confidence Bevil had, he didn't have clarity about his purpose beyond this service. He often took out his Bible for comfort. It strengthened his resolve to leave it in God's hands.

Richard enjoyed the humor of his comrades in between the onslaught of artillery, looked to the safety of his company, and enjoyed unexpected gifts. The gunfire frightened the wildlife, but he still listened for the bird's song in the morning, and the nocturnal symphony of the summer nights when the sounds of war grew quiet. He found freedom in the moonlight.

Freedom from the trench came near the end of July. Other troops took their place. The stress of the trench and the impending threat of the Federals exploding gunpowder stores under their lines had wearied all. After the corporal confirmed all of the men in Richard's company had exited the trench with all their gear, he called them into line. A more raggedy bunch he'd never seen, but they'd survived.

They marched in a southeast direction to a camp outside Petersburg.

Dehydration and hunger showed in their parched skin and evident fatigue, so he dismissed his men to a well-deserved respite.

The rest in the shade of the trees and direct access to a fresh stream of water renewed his outlook. Bevil flopped down beside him.

"Corporal Henry—I take it you have already reported to your sergeant."

Bevil opened one eye. "Indeed, I have, Sergeant Cushman. All is well in my company, and—I'm told— also in the rest of the First Texas ranks."

"Sergeant!"

Richard bolted to his feet and met the private scurrying toward him. "Look at you—you recovered from your wounds."

"I did." His hometown friend shrugged off his worn knapsack and reached inside it. "Hope I didn't lose it. This thing has so many holes I'm about done with it. I'm thinking of using my haversack or blanket roll for everything."

"Others have done it."

Richard waited while his friend rummaged a little more.

A crumpled letter emerged.

"Here you are." The young man grinned. "My cousin lives near here in Virginia, and your pa sent it enclosed in a letter my father sent. They let me recuperate. Anyway, it arrived before I left yesterday. I reported in with the captain while you were still in the trench, so am I good with you also?"

Richard smiled. "You are, Private." He held out his hand. "Let's have the letter."

The private handed it to Richard. "Hope it's all good tidings."

Bevil slung his arm over the shoulder of the returning soldier. "Let's catch up while he reads." He winked.

Richard's heart raced. He took a drink of water from his refreshed canteen and sat on the nearest log.

Unfolding the three pages, he read:

My son,

I hope this letter finds you well. From your last letter, as well as what has been shared by others and the sparse news reaching us, I have delayed my response.

Your tidings fell hard on our hearts in the delivery. I am sure the experience of them fell harder on yours.

If you have not heard, General Steele crossed our great Ouachita River at Rockport by pontoon bridge and camped a day here this spring. Our farms and homes are less well-supplied, but we endured it.

Our greater hardship has been the lack of rain. A drought has fallen hard on those who remain here.

From what I understand, somewhat of a drought of Confederate rations and supplies has reached you. So in many ways, you can feel our hunger and we can feel some of yours. I'm sure there is no way for us to identify with all you've endured.

When I came home, I was afraid I'd seen but a glimpse of what loomed over the horizon for my friends and family remaining. I have discussed rejoining the company, but the doctor feels I'd be asking to be shot with my current gait. Many have lost an entire leg with an injury such as mine. I praise the Lord for His great mercy on me.

I wanted you to know Marc and John are still alive but remain imprisoned by the Yanks at Ft. Delaware. Captain Richards remains with them. They too endure conditions worse than can be shared in letters. One man who did obtain release wrote his family before starting home.

I want to hear their experience with my own ears, and all here await their return as well as yours, and the number remaining in The Third's Company F.

Your mother, sisters, and I pray this great conflict will soon end and hope for a victorious outcome.

Richard shut his eyes. He'd seen the local people share freely with them and had also benefitted from foraging. The desperate need of soldiers for basic items sometimes dismissed the needs of civilians. None of it seemed justified when he read of the impact on his own family. The respective governments should supply their troops if they wanted them to fight. What had started out well and timely had no basis in their present state.

The men he fought with made every bit of it worthwhile. Their shared belief in the Confederate cause—for the rights of their states, their independence, and their families—bonded them. He knew some held varied beliefs regarding slavery, but regardless of these views, this war had changed things. It had changed him.

The unique aspect of staring into the eyes of a man who'd once been a fellow-countryman and seeing an enemy still gave him pause on occasion. He lifted an eyebrow and crossed his arms, resting the pages of the letter against his upper arm.

Of course, the sound of incoming artillery dissolved such a hesitation and refocused him with expediency on such occasions. Ironic humor lifted one side of his mouth.

He shook his head and uncrossed his arms and then shifted the pages. A half a page of feminine script. A few lines indeed, but beholding them meant more than any letter he'd read since the war began. He'd asked the burial detail to gather the letters and personal items from Jenny's pa's haversack before they buried him in the joint grave with the others. Out of honor, he had refused to read any of the letters and had mailed them along with two of the three personal items found. He'd addressed the packet to Jenny and hoped it had reached her.

No, he'd refused to read the letters she'd addressed to her father. Those words weren't his to read. But this page—meant for him by his Jenny's hand—he could read.

Richard,

Your parents have afforded me the freedom to write to you with their blessing. I must admit being nervous, but in another way not at all. Our childhood friendship grew without effort and budded into something with promise and hope for unfurling petals. The war halted the graceful transformation blooming, but it hasn't died. No, my memories of your many kindnesses and protection from the cruelty of others resulted in a beautiful amalgamation.

He stopped. What did that word mean? He knew he had his mother to thank for her knowledge of it—all of those books her relatives shared with them. Still, it sounded like a good thing. He wished Colonel Manning was still here instead of in a Yankee prison. He'd know what the word meant. Squinting, he struggled to make out the next smudged sentence.

You asked me if my affections have changed for you. Yes, they have.

His breath caught. He read it again.

Yes, they have. They've deepened and my fondness has grown. My hand is waiting for you and yours alone.

I remember you in my prayers each day. Do your duty with all your might and come home once it's over.

Ever yours,

Jenny

Moisture filled his eyes for the first time in months. He whispered, "I'm trying, Jenny." He blinked and read the postscript.

Thank you for the packet of my pa's things. His pipe and the tintype of my mother continue to bring me comfort.

He read her words again, folded the letter, and bowed his head. "Help me, Lord."

Reaching inside his haversack, he retrieved the treasured object he'd found in Jenny's pa's sack. He stacked it on top of his letter.

The log rolled underneath him. "Whoa!" He toppled, face forward. Laughter filled the air. He lifted his head and turned to find a group of Texans, including Bevil behind him. He scrambled to his feet and gathered his scattered treasures. His heart pounded.

He placed the letter on the log, then unwrapped and opened the small case holding the ambrotype of Jenny. He shut his eyes in relief. It wasn't broken.

The laughter subsided.

Richard rewrapped the case in the protective piece of tent canvas and slid it back in his haversack.

The men hadn't meant any harm, but still, he had to address it. He grabbed the letter and faced them.

"Good thing the ground is dry. I'd recommend guard duty for each of you if you'd muddied these." He shook the pages of his letter at them.

Bevil clasped one hand to his heart and held up the other. "On my honor, I checked the ground conditions."

Joe pushed him. "Did not."

Bevil returned the push. "You just didn't see me."

The other two laughed. "Maybe, but it doesn't matter. Your captain is looking for you, Sergeant."

Richard tucked the letter in his haversack. "Be glad I'm not your sergeant." He hurried to his captain. Orders determined they'd be in reserve here for about a week or so awaiting further orders.

How he wanted all the men left in the brigade to survive, to make it home. He'd never known better men. Sure, some found them a ragged and boisterous group. He grinned. The loyalty and fighting spirit of his friends remained unmatched in his heart. He'd do everything within his purview as a sergeant to lift morale and support his men.

For now, he knew General Lee's one focus—Richmond must not fall. They had to protect this jewel of the South.

Chapter Eighteen

The months churned away—a summer of drought and a lean autumn. Jenny listened to the two letters Richard had written to his father describing the Army of Northern Virginia's skirmishes in defense of Richmond in and around Petersburg, Deep Bottom, Fort Gilmer, Fort Harrison, and New Market Heights. He also described incidents on many roads, such as the Charles City Road, Darbytown Road, and the Williamsburg Road. Jenny sought a map of Virginia, but she gave up trying to track them, overwhelmed by the sheer amount of information.

The tone of the letters indicated Richard's resolve remained, but in October he described an intense battle earlier in the month wherein they had lost their brigade commander, Brigadier General John Gregg. The tone of his words changed in that last letter.

Listening to Richard's father read the letter, Jenny sensed a bit of despondency. Richard wrote of his and other officer's endeavors to boost the men's morale, but some still left the ranks. The Yanks had disrupted the supply lines to a devastating degree. Richard equated the lack of rations and persistent hunger to an enemy as aggressive as the blue coats they fought. Near the end of October, their division continued picket duty and building breastworks—temporary fortifications. The Texas Brigade sat on another road, the Williamsburg Road waiting for the healthier and better-nourished enemy.

The sheer magnitude of his situation overwhelmed her. Her mind had started ignoring any details of potential engagements, which may or may not manifest, or the actual fighting when they did. She wanted to talk to Richard face-to-face.

Jenny had longed for him to write her again, but he didn't. He did write one line, "Tell Jenny I am glad we are in agreement." She smiled at least twice a day as she repeated those words to herself.

In contrast, the army's dire need of supplies distressed her. With their own home front supply issues and inflation of prices, along with the results of the drought, Jenny could understand Richard's view of hunger as a great enemy, but she couldn't imagine having to fight like a soldier under those conditions.

She saw the gauntness of the soldiers who'd passed through the Rockport area but knew the challenges in Virginia differed. Due to the Federal's control of the Mississippi, destruction of railroads, and lack of imports from the rest of the world who had decided not to help the Confederacy, the Army of Northern Virginia faced even worse conditions. A prayer lingered on her lips with almost every breath these days.

The families had challenges to face within their own state. Mr. Cushman said to expect a new disruption every day. If it didn't come, give thanks, but if it did, face it head-on or step around it.

The biggest autumn disturbance in the Cushman yard arrived after lunch in early November. She opened the door to find a boy she remembered from school holding a bouquet of autumn leaves wrapped with a ribbon. His family had returned to Rockport last week.

"Is Florence home?"

"Good afternoon, Arnold."

The freckled topography of the youth's face scrunched into a distasteful frown. "I'd prefer you to refer to me as Mr. Beasley. After all, I am almost sixteen years old."

Jenny bit her lip.

Florey stepped around her and out onto the porch. She rolled her eyes and crossed her arms. "You've gone loco, Arnold Beasley. Living with your relatives has given you an inflated view of society here. You'd better wait until our soldiers come home before you call yourself a man."

He held out the odd bouquet. "It's never too early to court you."

"No!" Florence kept her arms crossed.

Jenny appraised the redness of Arnold's face—an anger matching the red in his hair. Their community had too many people with a nod to their Irish heritage and temperaments. The combination of two such individuals courting gave Jenny trepidations. Of course, each had a unique personality. Jenny balanced Richard's hotter temperament with her own calmer one. Matt could have balanced Florence. But Arnold? Never.

The young man dropped his offering to the ground. "*I* am here. Matt isn't coming home. You're lucky to have someone to call on you."

Dawn appeared in the doorway. "The war isn't over, *Mr.* Beasley. You might be conscripted yet."

"I'm too young."

"Exactly. So was Matt, but he went anyway."

An almost cruel expression appeared on his face. He opened his mouth.

"Don't say another word, Arnold." Dawn stepped through the door, joining them on the porch. "Go home. I'll tell my parents you called on us."

"Your pa will hear from mine." Arnold scurried down the steps.

Florey picked up the ribbon-tied autumn leaves and hurried after him, flinging them in the wake of his departure. "Don't come back until you have the courage to talk to my pa yourself—if you dare!". She whipped around, eyes wide. "Why did I say that?" Without waiting for a response, she spun toward the road. "I mean—don't come back at all."

Arnold raced down the road.

Her friend kicked at the ground, stirring the edge of her skirt. "He didn't hear me, did he?"

Jenny met her eyes and shrugged.

Alice wandered out of the house. "Are we finished with schooling for today, Dawn?"

Another effect of war. It had forced them to complete schooling at home. Dawn, Jenny, and even Florey had surpassed all the lessons in the old textbooks left in town, leaving Alice as the only one still studying at the insistence of her mother. The others in the community learned what they could at home, but some abandoned their schooling, having parents who couldn't read or write.

Mrs. Bailey had asked Dawn if she'd consider teaching a couple of mornings a week at their church building, but Mr. Cushman preferred to keep her home. Some days Will and Jack came by and joined the lessons. Jenny suspected they came to see Alice more than to learn, but Jack still managed to devour every book he received. She suspected he came for both.

If this war continued much longer, they'd all leave childhood behind. She hoped the victorious end came soon.

Dawn sighed. "Did you finish your spelling practice?"

Alice's blue eyes twinkled. "I did, but I don't know if I did them right. You need to check 'em."

Dawn patted her hair bun and then smoothed strands of hair away from her face, adjusting the combs on the sides of her middle part.

Jenny wondered about her beautiful friend's hopes and dreams. Dawn kept those things to herself. What did it hurt to ask? "Are you concerned about Marc?" Jenny watched for a blush or a fluster but saw none.

Dawn's voice softened. "Of course, I am. As you know, he requested to spend time with me before they left for war." She stared off for a moment at a bird who called from the tree in front of the house. "But he pulled back a couple of weeks before they left. He said they should be back soon, but just in case, he would not have me waiting." She wrapped an arm around the porch post. "I don't know. Marc and I will always be friends, but I'm not sure marriage to each other is best."

Florey laughed, coming up the steps. "That's plumb silly. Everyone knows you two are a pair."

Dawn scrunched her nose. "Who's *everyone*?" She placed a hand on her hip. "Has anyone heard from them?"

Florey scrunched her brow. "Who?"

Jenny laughed. "Marc and John."

Florey placed her hands behind her back and started whistling. "Not exactly, but Mrs. Wilkins said Mr. Johnson received a letter from a captain in prison with them, but he won't share it. He told her all he could say was prison was horrible, but the captain had found a way to assure him things would improve."

How odd. Jenny wanted to read the letter, but if Mr. Johnson felt it might be best for no one else to know, he would stay quiet.

Chapter Nineteen

Fort Delaware Prison, Pea Patch Island

Captain Boyd Richards stared at the courier. His traitorous uncle's persistence might be rewarded today—for the sake of his friends who lay dying of illness in their barracks. The leaky barracks. The overcrowded barracks. The—

"Do you have a reply today, Captain Richards?" The sneer of a question awaited his answer.

Boyd heaved a breath, the defeat eating at his insides. "Yes. I—we will accept my uncle's offer and conditions."

The courier's eyebrows lifted. "Well, well—"

"Don't start crowing in victory, sir. This is not the surrender of our hearts."

The man held out the paper and dipped the pen. Boyd sat in the chair at the small table, signing the oath of allegiance—once so disdained none would take it—and signed his name.

Within an hour, his two best friends, too weak to place more than a mark on the page, agreed to something he assured them they should. The head of the prison had him sign his friends' full names for clarification on the bottom of the pages. He'd betrayed their trust and that of their beloved brigade. At this point, the oath might be the only thing saving John and Marc's lives.

His uncle, a plantation owner and keeper of slaves, had sold his allegiance two years ago. From what Boyd could deduce, the man had worked for both the North and the South for his own gain. One side or the other should have shot such a dog, in Boyd's opinion.

A few months after arriving at Fort Delaware after Gettysburg, a courier started appearing every three months with his uncle's entreaty to take the oath and go home to Nancy and Sam. He'd refused.

Even though this prison had advantages over many of the other Union ones, the conditions destroyed many men. The men housed in the barracks had established their groups like small communities with political speeches made at intervals. Each revealed the state of his fellow prisoners' minds. The watchful eyes of sentinels kept them in check with the threat of being shot for breaking the rules, including a strict bedtime.

The cold, damp prison conditions and lack of necessities confined many to their bunks or sent them to the hospital. They'd all eaten rats. John's leg wounds had healed, and he'd kept his leg, but under these conditions, the giant of a man remained depleted.

Marc's early defiance had brought punishment in the first few months, when no talk of being exchanged came. Boyd didn't know until months later the cause of it. He had told the first courier he'd never leave without his friends, and he knew they'd never take the oath. His uncle had deemed the idea of him returning to fight unacceptable but made sure Boyd received clothing and extra things. Boyd had refused or sold many of them, requesting his uncle send provisions to his wife, son, and brother instead.

The recent dismal news from the battlefront contributed to his present decision to sign the oath in the face of a bitter late autumn and winter. Even leaving here held no guarantees. His friends still might die, but he had to try. He hoped they'd forgive him later. If the South somehow found victory, he'd take responsibility for today's actions. But he could never look into the eyes of the other men in the brigade again.

Boyd thought about Marc's friend from home— Arty, a Third Lieutenant from Witherspoon's Cavalry, who'd arrived after being in a couple of different prisons. He kept telling them he had a friend who'd find him and take him home. They'd laughed, but he stuck to his belief even to the day last week when they'd moved him out for transfer to Johnson's Island in Ohio.

Thankful the men in the bunks nearest him slept or were out in the prison yard, Boyd took stock of Marc and John's limited possessions. While the courier headed to the warden of the prison's office, Boyd gathered their belongings in his haversack, including the small items he'd whittled for Nancy and Sam.

He had written them but had requested Nancy and Ben not send any response. Boyd didn't want the soldiers who read through their letters to find any news of Texas, his community, or his family. He grabbed his last page of stationery and scribbled a brief letter to Marc's father.

The sound of tramping feet lifted his head. The courier appeared.

"There is a wagon across the moat to take us to a boat. The hospital has settled your friends in the back of it. Although I'll not discuss our planned route in detail, I will say to expect a stop at City Point, Virginia."

"But I thought the exchanges had stopped. What do I tell my friends?"

"Don't question things, Mr. Richards. There are several islands we could also stop by, but depending on how your friends are doing, we might surpass them. Our goal is to take you to City Point in Virginia and then on to Mississippi. I have orders to leave you there. There is a family who will allow you to rest, and then they will see you to Louisiana, but you'll have to find your way home from there.'"

The sentinels escorted him to the Sally Port entrance. He kept his head down, not daring to make eye contact with any of his fellow prisoners.

What had he done? He hoped John and Marc forgave him; he didn't know if he could forgive himself. If his friends lived, at least he'd attain some justification.

His feet trod the wooden boards, and he left the castle-like structure of misery. *Justification.* He wondered how Aunt Elizabeth felt about his uncle's activities. If she even knew. How had she handled things at the plantation? Were Martha and Daniel, his childhood friends, even there?

Regardless of the war's outcome, he wanted them free and living close to him, Nancy, and Ben. Friendship knew no shades of the politics of Blue or Gray, but the war had changed everything.

~

Georgia

Elizabeth Richards stared at the backs of the departing couple—former slaves—from the steps of the large plantation house. She'd seen to their marriage and provided what she could for their travel. Then she wished them well. Her nephews had grown up playing with them. Both she and her husband had thought the childhood friendships would pass. Events had proven the opposite to be true.

Nancy never ceased to ask about them in her letters. In fact, her last letter had prompted the actions Elizabeth had taken tonight—actions completed without her husband's approval. He may never notice their absence. After all, she'd been left to deal with all of it these last couple of years. Even the terror of Sherman's march. Part of her might resent her husband for many years.

Elizabeth turned to the man standing next to her— one of the men her husband had left to protect her. Men she suspected came from the North. "You are to take a friend and follow the pair until they reach Louisiana. I have made arrangements for their safe conduct from there to the farm of my nephew. They must never know you gave them safe passage. Dear Nancy needs the help of friends. They are the best I can send, and they've agreed it's where they want to go."

The usually quiet man nodded. "It's a good thing you've done."

She smirked when he tipped his hat. He must be a Yankee.

The cold bite of the February evening seeped through her dress. At least the travelers shouldn't face the heavy rains they'd endured the previous month. She turned with a broad sweep of her hooped skirt and made her way into the house.

Chapter Twenty

Surrounded, starving, and surrendered, Richard hung his head.

A sense of foreboding had lurked in the shadows ever since they boarded the train at Richmond on the second night in April. Their departure came on the heels of the Confederate government's departure from Richmond due to the approach of the Federals.

After disembarking from the train, they marched to the north side of the Appomattox River. The commanders intended to guard against the Federals crossing there. They didn't cross, so the Texas Brigade marched again before midnight.

None of that or the rest of their journey prepared them for today. Standing in a line reminiscent of a fingernail-shaped sliver of the moon—on April 9th—Richard swallowed hard and stayed behind the crude breastworks. Somberness overtook their ranks after a stalled advance and a blocked retreat.

"Do you believe it's true?" Bevil whispered in the wake of the afternoon pronouncement by some teamsters. "Several soldiers called them liars."

Richard lifted his head. "I feel it must be."

Confirmation came from their commanders, but denial reigned until General Lee rode down the road and told them they could go home.

Richard sank to the ground, tears coursing down his face.

The night fell in a curtain of despondency heavy with despair and hunger.

"Hey, Johnny Reb," a hesitant voice called out of the darkness. All the heads of those who shared the campfire with Richard turned.

Richard could see a Yank at the edge of a spill of firelight. He swallowed, seeing shadows behind the man. He stood. "What do you want, Billy Yank?"

The man approached opening his haversack. "We want to share our rations."

Dumbstruck, Richard swallowed. His stomach, which had long ceased to grumble, responded in kind. His eyes met Sam's, who nodded. Richard stepped forward. "That's friendly of you and much appreciated. Where are you from?"

"Illinois."

A man from behind him said, "Ohio."

Only God could have arranged something like this. He'd never forget it. One of his journaling soldiers should write it down for history.

A damp rain and cold temperatures sickened their spirits more during the next two days.

On April 12th, the line to surrender their arms moved like a doomed snail. Some had rather destroy the guns than to surrender them, but one of the captains took action to correct this inclination. Richard's hand lingered on the barrel of his musket-rifle for a long moment before he leaned it up against the stack and placed his cartridge box beside it.

He still felt like a soldier. Signing the oath of allegiance for his parole slip meant he couldn't be a soldier for the Confederacy. Lee had surrendered the Army of Northern Virginia, but General Johnston had not yet surrendered the Army of Tennessee, nor had the other remaining generals surrendered their armies. So, the Confederacy still existed, but all knew its shallow breaths had no means by which to revive itself. In Richard's mind, General Johnston's activities no longer mattered as Lee had surrendered. The remaining members of their brigade had a long journey ahead of them.

Someone touched his arm. He turned to find Bevil at his elbow. "I might write you when I get home."

A lump formed in Richard's throat. He swiped the end of his nose and swallowed hard. "I'd like that. Any plans?"

"I'll go see how Texas is doing, and I need to see my parents, but I'm thinking about going out west—to the territories."

"Away from all the politics?"

Bevil grinned. "You know me well."

"Mark my words, those places will have their own."

"You're right, but I'm more focused on finding God's path."

He offered him the best smile he could. "I pray you find it." When Bevil started to turn, Richard grabbed his elbow. "Live it for two."

Bevil winked. "Matt's always with me."

The bittersweet goodbyes with the rest of the Texans left him standing with what remained of the Third Arkansas. They watched the Texans march away together for the last time.

Each company gathered, many agreeing they should go through Chattanooga and Memphis, but others considered routes through Greenville to Nashville, Tennessee, and then making their way to Little Rock and then home.

Richard calculated between 130 to 150 men marched on the roads, starting toward Arkansas that day. Those in his own company F numbered fewer than the count of two hands.

Their journey brought talk of those no longer with them. Stories, memories, and determination carried them to Arkansas. Every time they had to stop and have their papers checked or saw burned homes with smokeless chimneys, the call of home grew louder. Richard could almost hear his mother calling him for supper. They kept moving, only stopping when they grew tired.

The news of President Lincoln's assassination on April 14th and consequential death on the 15th reached them along the way.

He and the men traveling with him reached Arkansas in mid-May. Some of the other companies had diverged paths from them or made stops along the way, delaying their return home until June. That thought brought a smile. June to June in leaving and coming home seemed poetic, but their group wanted to return home as soon as possible.

A disheartening sight greeted them, the ravages of war, drought, and pillaging evident.

As Company F neared Rockport, Carl Wilkins broke off from them and headed to his farm. They waved to him, then screams stopped Richard. He held up a halting hand. They'd surrendered their guns but not their knives.

Those 'Arkansas Toothpicks' appeared.

Richard got his bearings. "It's coming from near Jenny's place. She's not living there."

They circled off the road and crept through the trees behind the cabin. Two men stood in front of the cabin holding what looked like meat from the smokehouse.

Screams emanated from the cabin, and a man exited the door carrying an emaciated young woman. Richard started to move, but his lieutenant shook his head.

The woman kicked and screamed all the way into the middle of the yard.

"This is the squaw girl I told you two about. We'll finish with her and go back to that farm for the rest." He dropped the woman and slapped her across the face. "You, hush."

She turned her head. *Could that be Jenny?*

His lieutenant nodded. They moved with stealth precision, splitting so they came up along both sides of the cabin.

A steel-cold anger coursed through Richard. He tightened his grip on his knife.

The screams stopped, and Jenny went limp. The men gathered around her.

"I think she's dead."

"Naw."

The lead guerrilla reached for his pants. "It doesn't matter."

Richard and the rest moved, coming up behind the men so quick and quiet they had the points of their blades against the men's necks before they could react.

"Oh, yes, it matters," the lieutenant said.

Richard dropped to his knees, scooping Jenny into his arms. She lashed out like a wildcat. He held her tighter. "It's me, Jenny. It's Richard." She pummeled his chest with her fists. "It's Richard."

Her eyes widened, losing the sheen of wild, unseeing desperation. Her raised fists froze and then fell open to rest on his chest. "Richard?" Her eyes searched his face and filled with tears. She buried her face against his neck and sobbed.

Over her head, he nodded at his friends who'd trussed up the men. They disappeared back into the woods, dragging their prisoners with them. Richard had no idea who'd they turn them over to, but he had no doubt they could figure it out just fine.

Sam waved. "I put the meat back in the smokehouse. I confess I took a taste." He grinned.

Richard's throat constricted as Sam disappeared over the rise behind Jenny's cabin. A horse nickered. Richard turned. A wagon moved toward him. He lowered Jenny to the ground, placing his worn haversack under her head.

"Whoa." The man reined the horse. He removed his hat and jumped down.

Richard noted his uneven gait. "Pa."

The man hobbled forward. "You didn't tell me you made Sergeant."

He sniffed and compressed his lips "Slipped my mind." Richard threw his arms around his father, closing his eyes. The first embrace of home. His pa's reciprocal hug tightened and then released.

Pa stepped back and glanced at Jenny. "Is she asleep?"

Richard squatted beside her. "Appears to be, but her ma taught her how to play possum. We ran off some guerrillas."

"We?" Pa lifted his eyebrow.

Richard nodded. "What's left of Company F is home."

His father bent over Jenny. "Sweet girl?" No response. "Let's get her home."

Richard gathered her up, haversack and all.

Pa held the horse's bridle as Richard laid her in the back of the wagon and started around to the front, but stopped, returning to the back. He hopped in beside her.

"Hold the horse steady a while longer, Pa." He knelt in the wagon bed and scooped her up again, holding her against him as he scooted to sit behind the wagon bench. "We're ready."

Pa took his seat and slapped the reins.

Richard leaned his head against the back of the seat. He inhaled. Home smelled the same. He looked down at Jenny's gaunt face. She'd bloomed into a young woman. Hungry days had sharpened the angles of her high cheekbones. He lifted his hand, longing to trace them but stopped. He'd wait.

"Pa?" His voice caught.

"We're home." Pa stopped the wagon and climbed down. "Jenny will be fine." He patted Richard's shoulder from the edge of the wagon. The volume of his voice increased. "Ladies, this young man helped Jenny. Anybody know him?"

Richard lifted his head. His mother and sisters stood on the porch.

Florey—it had to be her—ran down the steps, lifted her skirt, and piled into the wagon. Yep, Florey. Her gray eyes, so like his own, searched his bearded face. She yanked off his tattered hat and kissed him on the head. "Nigh time you got home." Tears welled up and spilled, streaming down her face.

Jenny stirred. Her eyes fluttered and opened.

Florey, being Florey, didn't wait. "Jenny, are you okay?"

Jenny's gaze collided with his. It almost felled him. He grinned. She pushed away and sat up. "I dreamed of you."

He winked and scooted past her. His mother hurried down the steps. She wouldn't burst into tears. He knew her, but she felt things deep.

"Richard." His mother stood at the foot of the steps, "It took longer than you thought."

He took her hands in his and squatted a bit to meet her eye-level. "It did, Ma."

Without warning, she pulled at his worn shirt and thrust her hand inside, touching the scar on his shoulder. She closed his shirt. "It's healed."

He touched his forehead to hers. "It has."

She shut her eyes and then wriggled her nose. "You need a bath."

Alice giggled. He took the steps two at a time and grabbed his youngest sister, tickling her.

His mother clicked her tongue. "Richard Cushman, she's too old for that."

Alice laughed, hugging him. "No, I'm not."

He didn't care. He'd missed so much.

Dawn. He appraised his beautiful blonde sister. "You're grown."

She smiled. "So are you."

"I'm still older."

"You are. Glad you came home. I didn't like being the eldest these past few years."

"The least I could do."

She hugged him. He glanced toward the road.

"Have you heard from Marc or John?"

She pushed away from him. "No." She opened the door. "Ma's right. I'm preparing you a bath."

Pa slid his fingers under his suspenders. "Give the boy some air. You ladies see to what food we might have. He looks hungry."

Jenny's hands went to her face. "Did they steal the meat?"

"Almost, but it's back where it belongs." He scratched his head. "If you've been here, how'd the meat get to your pa's smokehouse?"

"It's not as close to the road." Jenny came up the steps to the porch.

It took Richard a minute. Realization dawned and his gaze shifted to his pa. "The soldiers cleared yours before?"

His pa pushed back his hat. "Indeed. Come help in the barn."

Jenny hesitated at the door.

He turned to her and couldn't look away.

His pa cleared his throat.

Jenny ducked her head and disappeared inside.

Richard ambled down the steps.

Chapter Twenty-One

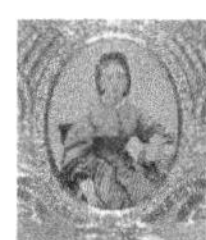

The barn cat pounced at something at the edge of
the barn. Jenny laughed.

"That's the best sound of the morning."

She whirled around almost dropping the egg in her
hand. Her eyes found Richard's chest—his clean shirt
covering it—and lifted her eyes to his face. After he
bathed and ate last night, he'd gone straight to bed.
Mrs. Cushman had insisted. The recollection of his
height being less in memory and more in reality, she
tilted her head back. "You shaved."

She could see his whole face, and what a
handsome one—not a tittle of hair anywhere. Light
creases appeared beside his eyes, but otherwise he—
"You look like you did when you marched away in
'61."

"Do I?" He wrinkled his nose.

She brushed her finger to the edge and below his
eye. "Almost."

He turned and extended his arms across the rail of the corral, propping his boot on the bottom rail.

"Do those still fit?"

He kicked his heel against the rail. "A little snug but not bad. Shoes have met with such scarcity, I am more than glad Ma kept these for me. My old pants don't fit. I'll stick with these for now. Ma and Dawn said they could combine the material from a couple of them to make me a new pair."

"Is this what you want to talk about?"

He raised an eyebrow. "Not really. You?"

"No."

"We have many challenges in front of us." He straightened and turned, hanging his arms over the top rail. "There's a house to rent close to the river."

"I know." She grabbed the rail beside him. "We've both faced challenges." She turned her head, studying the profile of his face. "How close?"

He turned his head, chuckling. "Pa says the river will wash the house away in a flood, but I think it might only wash the back of the barn."

She wrinkled her nose and smiled. "Sounds lovely. How will we pay for it?"

"We could sell your pa's cabin and land."

Sadness filled her. "No, I'd like to keep it. Let's live there."

Richard's eyes locked with hers. "Let's, but only until I can earn enough to pay a regular rent, or we can stay here until then."

Jenny retrieved another egg and placed it in the basket. "Are we agreeing or just talking?"

"Agreeing, but . . . you'd better run those eggs in to Ma. Ask her to excuse you."

She hurried in with the eggs. "Richard wants to agree with me."

Mrs. Cushman stopped pouring the milk. "Oh, he does?" She smiled. "It's taken him the entire war to say it. Get out there with my blessing."

Mr. Cushman took a sip of coffee. "Mine too. We'll return to polite manners soon enough."

Dawn checked the pan cooking the breakfast eggs and smiled.

Jenny found Alice and Florey outside with Richard. She joined them. "I'm here."

Alice giggled and ran to the house, but Florey looked ready to cry.

"What's wrong?"

Richard put his arm around his sister. "We were talking about Matt. I'm not quite ready to discuss the battles face-to-face with you ladies. Mr. Wilkins was—anyway, he knows about Matt's last words. I'm just not ready, but Florey, if he were here—"

Florey didn't stay to hear him finish. She ran toward the road instead of the house.

Jenny ran after her. "Florey, you can't go to your special spot. It's still not safe. Give him time. Let him be at home and not at war for a breath."

"I know. Forgive my selfishness. It's just I . . . I have so many questions."

"Some questions will never have answers."

"I know." Florey grabbed her hands and squeezed them. "Go back to my brother. I'll go inside."

Once Florey disappeared into the house, Richard walked toward Jenny and offered his arm. She took it and stared up at him. "Some people are returning, but the town is not as you remember it. It's best for us to stay close to the house."

"Care to walk by the old fishing hole?"

Jenny laughed. "That isn't deserted. We're liable to find Will or Jack there."

He stopped.

"What is it?"

"How will they feel about me being home when Marc isn't yet?"

Jenny squeezed his arm. "Of course, they want Marc home, as well as John, but they want you home too. Is Sam home?"

"Yes. Matt knew him better than I did before the war, but that boy—young man—is tough. He'll make something of himself." Richard moved ahead, she in tandem with him. "Have they talked about Matt?"

"Yes. He wrote to Will even more than his family."

"I didn't know that. He kept quiet and steady, but after Gettysburg, he really grew to be a man." He covered her hand, holding it in place on his arm. "He loved Florey, but I can't tell her what he said."

Why on earth not? She took a deep breath. "I don't understand."

"She knows in her own way, but it's something I want to save until she's ready to marry. It might make the difference in her choice."

"Why not tell her now?"

"It's too soon. Right now, she doesn't want to consider anyone else, but she's getting to the age."

Part of Jenny wanted to remind him of her own age—but wait. She stopped. "Are you really here?" The wonder of it overwhelmed her heart. His dear face. Tears spurted.

"Oh, my, Jenny." He pulled her to a large rock next to the fishing hole. "Sit with me."

They sat. His eyes searched hers. He cradled her face in his hands.

"Will you do me the honor—marry me?"

Her voice betrayed her, so she nodded.

He pulled her against his chest, his protective, warm arms holding her. "You're my answer and my stay."

Tears filled her eyes. The Good Lord had confirmed this for them. She sighed. Complete contentment and peace filled her.

He pulled back, taking her hands in his. "I don't have anything right now, but we will overcome whatever is ahead. We've made it through *these* years. I'll find a way—with God's help."

His gray eyes flickered with the spark she hadn't seen since he'd returned home. Joy kissed happiness in that moment. "Of course, we will."

"My tender affections for you are offered with an abiding love this day."

She touched his cheek. "I love you, Richard Cushman. I always have."

Laughter sounded on the other side of the pond.

"Looks like you two need a chaperone."

Jenny jumped to her feet. Will and Jack stood on the other side.

Richard bolted to his feet and circled the pond. "Looks like you two need a dunking." He grabbed them by the back of their shirts and flung them both in the water. Well, he flung Jack and pushed Will. They came up sputtering. Richard threw his head back and laughed as they scrambled for the bank.

Jenny's heart rejoiced. He needed this. They all did.

Chapter Twenty-Two

The boys scrambled out and tackled him, just like they had done in younger days.

"You boys have gotten too big for this." Will had filled out more than Jack, but the passage of time had matured them as well. Both young men still held the wonder of boyhood. Richard didn't think he'd ever know that wonder again.

They shook the water from their hair and flopped down beside him.

"It's good to see you, Richard," Will said.

Jack grinned. "It sure is."

That boy resembled his oldest brother. "Jack, has anyone told you how much you're looking like Marc?"

Jenny had circled around to them. "He knows." She crossed her arms.

Will stood. "I'm sorry, Jenny. We should have gone home without interrupting you."

She patted his arm. "It's fine. At least he asked for my hand before you interrupted."

Jack crowed like a rooster. "We didn't just wake up yesterday. 'Sides, we saw Sam on the road early last evening. We knew you got home. Pa said you needed at least a night before we could come find you."

"Well, you found me." He hesitated, but he had to ask. "Have you heard from Marc?"

Will skipped a rock across the pond. "Not until last week, but one of his friends wrote our pa a couple of times."

"Who?"

"Some captain."

"Captain Boyd Richards?"

Jack elbowed Will. "Told you he'd know him."

"Are they still in prison?"

"Pa didn't know where they were until last week."

Richard had about lost patience. "Answer me. Are they still in prison?"

Will crossed his arms and lifted his chin "They're in Texas."

Richard hugged Jenny. "That's good. Is John with them?"

"Yep."

So the exchange system had started again. He didn't care how. "Are they on their way here?"

"Nope. They finally recovered from being sick." The boys stood and started backing away at Richard's frown. Will chewed on his bottom lip. "You'd better talk to Pa."

Confusion and irritation mixed within him. He rubbed his brow. "I think I'd better."

Jack broke away and ran, Will lumbering after him.

Jenny touched his shoulder. "I'm sure Marc and John will come home when they can."

Richard studied her beautiful face. "They're alive. That's what counts." He took her hand and lifted it to his lips. "I love you." *She'd said yes to him.* He'd ponder his absent friends later.

Yesterday's events replayed in his mind, but he refused to belabor them. God had brought him here in time to rescue her. His friends had helped. He knew the caliber of men in their brigade, their infantry, and company F. The members of the brigade, whether from Texas or Arkansas, had a firm bond. That's how they'd start their lives again, helping each other. His heart hammered and he hugged her. "We're going to be fine, Jenny."

If they announced the official end of the war, Richard had a feeling this Reconstruction the Federals spoke about may look different since Lincoln's death. Some said Johnson might honor Lincoln's plan, but as he and the others traveled home, they'd heard talk about the vengeful attitudes in Congress. It could take a long time before they'd readmit the states.

His heart yearned for the independence they'd paid for in blood but never won. He mourned for the destruction and loss. He hugged Jenny tight.

Pulling back, he lifted her chin. His eyes searched hers."Let's get married in August."

Jenny's eyes sparkled. "I agree."

How he loved her—much more than the freedom from battle the early nights away had provided. He'd made it home.

"God will see us through."

Her brown eyes radiated joy. "He already has."

Richard kissed her. The faces of every man who'd marched away with him on that June day so long ago played before his eyes. The laughing, proud faces of friends he'd never see again, as well as the handful of those battle-honed veterans who'd returned with him yesterday. He kissed her again for all of them.

THE END

Author's message to each reader:
Thank you for reading *Moonlight and Freedom.* Please leave a review on Amazon, Goodreads, BookBub, or other sites. I treasure your feedback. As this is the prequel to the post-Civil War series: *Home Always Beckons; Trails of Change; Sunbeams at Twilight; and A Compass of Stars in Your Eyes,* I hope you will read each book in this series. May God bless each of you.

Hugs,
Lana Lynne

Author's Bio

Lana Lynne is the author pen name of Lana Lynne Higginbotham in the fiction genre. She is a member of ACFW and the East Texas Christian Writers group. Lana balanced a career as a speech-language pathologist with her writing until late November 2019. A step of faith led her to step away from the role of SLP to spend more time with family and to focus on her writing. Lana's books are published by Winged Publications under the leadership of Cynthia Hickey. Her novels include *Home Always Beckons*: *A New Sunrise, Trails of Change*: *A New Sunset, Sunbeams at Twilight*: *A Life's Echo,* and *A Compass of Stars in Her Eyes*—a post-Civil War historical fiction romance series; the Whimsy's Heart Books: *Whimsy Michaels and Her Amazing Room* and *Stephen Michaels and His Upside-down Umbrella*—works of contemporary Christian fiction; *The Adventures of Bo Jack*—a historical fiction based on/inspired by a family member's childhood memories; *Picnics, Plays, and Autograph-Book Days*—a historical fiction novella based on/inspired by the author's maternal grandparents' 1920s love story; *Three Whistles Around the Bend*—a Firebird Book award-winning Christian historical fiction romance novella; *The Wildness of Spring,* a contemporary romance novella; and her newest release, *Moonlight and Freedom*. It is the prequel to the post-Civil War series started by her first book, *Home Always Beckons*: *A New Sunrise*.

Lana lives with her husband in East Texas. They are empty nesters and proud grandparents.

Books by Lana Lynne:

<u>Home Always Beckons: A New Sunrise</u>

<u>Trails of Change: A New Sunset</u>

<u>Sunbeams at Twilight: A Life's Echo</u>

<u>A Compass of Stars in Your Eyes</u>

<u>Whimsy Michaels and Her Amazing Room</u>

<u>The Adventures of Bo Jack</u>

<u>Picnics, Plays, and Autograph-Book Days</u>

<u>Three Whistles Around the Bend</u>

<u>Stephen Michaels and His Upside-Down Umbrella</u>

<u>The Wildness of Spring</u>

New Release:
Moonlight and Freedom

*[Non-fiction: now out of print due to prior publisher closing and with limited availability from third party sellers:
<u>Life Between the Letters: The Chuck and Mary Felder Story</u>

By Lana Lynne Higginbotham and Mary K. Felder.]

**Some of Lana's stories are also part of compilations and book sets from her publisher, Winged Publications.

How to Connect with Lana Lynne:

Follow Lana on:
Amazon
BookBub
Goodreads

Find Lana on Social Media Links:
Lana's personal Facebook

Lana's Author Facebook Page: Lana Lynne

X (Formerly known as Twitter)

Pinterest

LinkedIn

Instagram

Website: https://www.lanalynne.com/

Research Sources
Selected Bibliography for Further Reading

Author's Note:
There are no direct quotes from these sources in this story, but they have shaped the chronology of the historical events for the structure and background of my fictional novel. I have endeavored to write with historical accuracy. After completing extensive research, I have listed the sources I found essential to depict a valid historical background true to the history and people surrounding my characters. The places, events, and people joining my fictional characters in this novel are well-known. All interactions with my characters are fictitious in nature and from my imagination. The actual Civil War events interwoven in this story are based on available research. Any inadvertent errors or adjustments made for the purpose of this fictional account are my own. I have arranged the sources by type to make it easier for the reader.

A list of my fictional characters can be found in the front of the book to distinguish them from the historic Civil War figures and commanders mentioned. The real people I chose to name within the story are limited, given the scope of the Civil War. Within the confines of this story, there was no way to include an exhaustive recognition of all of the men involved on both sides. I have connected my fictional characters with key commanders and real Third Arkansas Infantry Regiment members, especially those in Company F, who would have encountered or known about the battles or actions in which they took part, but not all. This is a fictional novel and not a history book, but readers can find out more details about the actual history from the Selected Bibliography for Further Reading listed below:

BOOKS

Bailey, Ronald H. and the Editors of Time-Life Books. *The Bloodiest Day: The Battle of Antietam.* The Civil War. Alexandria, Virginia: Time-Life Books Inc., 1984. 5th printing, 1993.

Carson, Clarence B. *A Basic History of the United States, Vol-Book 3: The Sections and the Civil War 1826-1877.* Beth A. Hoffman, ed. consultant. Greenville, Alabama: American Textbook Committee, 1985.

Clark, Champ and the Editors of Time-Life Books. *Gettysburg: The Confederate High Tide.* The Civil War. Alexandria, Virginia: Time-Life Books Inc., 1985. 3rd Printing. Rev.ed. 1987.

Collier, Captain Calvin L. *"They'll Do To Tie To!" The Story of the Third Regiment, Arkansas Infantry C. S. A. (Book jacket title: They'll Do To Tie To! Hood's Arkansas Toothpicks, Third Arkansas Infantry Regiment- C. S. A.).* Little Rock: Eagle Press, 1959. 3rd Printing. 1988.

Dickens, Charles, *Oliver Twist.* (text from 1867 Charles Dickens edition). **Toronto, New**

York, London, Sydney: Bantam Books, Bantam Classic edition, 1981.

Evans, Gen. Clement A. Evans, ed; Dimitry, John, A. M. "Louisiana" and Harrell, Col. John M. "Arkansas" in *Confederate Military History: Vol. 10: Louisiana and Arkansas, A Library Of Confederate States History, In Thirteen Volumes, Written By Distinguished Men of the South, and Edited by Gen, Clement A Evans of Georgia . . . , Vol 10: Louisiana and Arkansas.* See esp. *Arkansas* section of two-book volume, Chap.1: 3-24; 8:194-222; 9: 223-247; 11: 284-325; 12: 326-376; in Biographical section: 414-416. United States of America, Secaucas, N. J.: The Blue and Gray Press, A Division of Book Sales, Inc., n.d. [ca.1960-1975] [Edition is a reprint of the original publication in Atlanta: Confederate Publishing Co.1899].

Foote, Shelby. *Stars in Their Courses: The Gettysburg Campaign June-July 1863.* Modern Library Edition. New York: The Modern Library, 1994.

Foote, Shelby. *The Civil War Narrative: Fredericksburg to Meridian.* New York: Civil War Library, Vintage Books, A Division of Random House, 1986. First published 1963 by Random House, Inc.

Goodspeed Publishing Company. *The Goodspeed Biographical and Historical Memoirs of Central Arkansas: Jefferson, Saline, Hot Spring, Pulaski, Garland, Lonoke, Perry, Faulkner, and Grant Counties.* Easley, South

Carolina: Southern Historical Press, New Material, 1978 by Rev. Silas Emmett Lucas Jr. Reprinted from 1889 edition in the private library of Mrs. Larry P. Clark, Little Rock, Arkansas. First Published, 1889 by Goodspeed Publishing Company as *Biographical and Historical Memoirs of Pulaski, Jefferson, Lonoke, Faulkner, Grant, Saline, Perry, Garland and Hot Spring Counties, Arkansas, Comprising A Condensed History of the State, A Number of Biographies of Distinguished Citizens of the Same, A Brief Description of each of the counties above named, and numerous Biographical Sketches of their Prominent Citizens, Illustrated.* See "Hot Spring County," Chapter 18: 319-360, and esp. 336-339. Chicago, Nashville and St. Louis: The Goodspeed Publishing Company, 1889.

Gottfried, Bradley M. *The Maps of Gettysburg: An Atlas of the Gettysburg Campaign, June 3-July 13, 1863.* Eldorado Hills, CA: Savas Beatie LLC, (black and white edition 2007) First Edition,Third Printing, Color edition, 2013.

Hawkins, Van. *Duty Bound: The Hyatt Brothers and Confederates of the Third Arkansas Infantry Regiment, Army of Northern Virginia, C. S. A.* Jonesboro, Arkansas: Arkansas State University, 2011.

Hempstead, Fay. *Historical Review of Arkansas: Its Commerce, Industry and Modern Affairs, Vol. 1.* Illustrated. Chicago: The Lewis Publishing Co., 1911. Reprinted from original edition from the private library of the Rev. S. Emmett Lucas Jr. Easley, South Carolina: Southern Historical Press: circa 1978.

Jaynes, Gregory and the Editors of Time-Life Books. *The Killing Ground: Wilderness to Cold Harbor.* The Civil War. Alexandria, VA.: Time-Life Books Inc., 1986, Second printing. Revised 1987.

Jordan, Robert Paul. *The Civil War.* Washington D.C.: National Geographic Society, 1969.

Knight, Rena Marie. *Additional Civil War Soldiers in Arkansas, Vol. 1, A-K: with Biographies, Narratives, Photos, and Illustrations,* Jacksonville, Arkansas: RMK Publishing Co., 2004: 160-161.

Polley, J. B. *Hood's Texas Brigade: Its Marches, Its Battles, Its Achievements.* New York and Washington: The Neale Publishing Co., 1910.

Powell, David A., and Cartography by Friedrichs, David A. *The Maps of Chickamauga: An Atlas of the Chickamauga Campaign, including the Tullahoma Operations. June 22-23, 1863,* El Dorado Hills, CA: Savas Beatie LLC, 2009; Third Edition, First Printing, 2015.

Robertson, James I. Jr. and the Editors of Time-Life Books. *Tenting Tonight: The Soldier's Life.* The Civil War. Alexandria, VA: Time-Life Books Inc.,1984.

The Editors of Time-Life Books. *Lee Takes Command: From Seven Days to Second*

Bull Run. The Civil War. Alexandria, VA: Time-Life-Books Inc., 1984; Third Printing, 1993.

Ural, Susannah J. *Hood's Texas Brigade: The Soldiers and Families of the Confederacy's Most Celebrated Unit.* Baton Rouge: Louisiana State University Press, 2017.

Wright, Gen. Marcus J., assisted by Col. Benjamin La Bree and James P. Boyd, A.M. *Official and Illustrated War Record: Embracing Nearly One Thousand Pictorial Sketches By the Most Distinguished American Artists of Battles by Land and Sea, Camp and Field Scenes, Insignia of Rank and Leading Characters In the Wars of the United States . . . . ,*Copyright Edward J. Stanley 1898. *Washington [D.C.],[Subscription only],*1899.

PERIODICALS

Erwin, John H. (Mr. Erwin notes origin of article: *Malvern Daily Record, August 19, 1977 in "Looking Back")* "Brief History of Hot Spring County, Arkansas." Editors: Mrs. J. H. Gibbs and Mrs. Fenton Stanley, *The Heritage* 5, Hot Spring County, Arkansas, Historical Society, 1978: 96-98.

Gibbs, Mrs. J. H. and Mrs. Fenton Stanley, eds. "Old Rockport Gets Two New Bridges." Editors: Mrs. J. H. Gibbs and Mrs. Fenton Stanley, *The Heritage* 7, Hot Spring County, Arkansas, Historical Society, 1980: 109-111.

Hot Spring County, Arkansas, Historical Society staff: Mr. John H. Erwin, ed. and Mrs. Jeannie Gibbs and Mrs. Bernice Roache, compilers, noted *The Arkansas Gazette Magazine Section,* June 7, 1936, as original place of publication. "Old Rockport Where the President Worships Wednesday." Editor: Mr. John H. Erwin, *The Heritage* 8, Hot Spring County, Arkansas, Historical Society. 1981: 109-115.

Source Unknown. "When Our Major Rivers Had No Bridges." Editor: Bonnie Dixon Stanley. *The Heritage* 24, Hot Spring County, Arkansas, Historical Society, 1997: 133.

Source Unknown. "You May Hear Some More about Rockport." Editor: Bonnie Dixon Stanley. *The Heritage* 24, Hot Spring County, Arkansas, Historical Society, 1997: 134.

Stacy, Bruce and with comments by Meyer H. Fishbein. "The History of Hot Spring County." Editor: Bonnie Dixon Stanley (Mrs. Fenton Stanley), *The Heritage* 4, Hot Spring County, Arkansas, Historical Society, 1977: 3,4.

Stanley, Bonnie Jean and Eugenia (Jeannie) Gibbs, eds. (Editors note reference for a portion of information to *Malvern Daily Record: 25th Edition,* 1941 and *50th Edition,* 1966.) T*he Heritage.* "Early Road of Hot Spring County," Editors: Bonnie Jean Stanley and Eugenia (Jeannie) Gibbs, *The Heritage* 2, Hot Spring County, Arkansas, Historical Society, 1971 (second edition 1980): 33-37.

Stanley, Bonnie Dixon, ed. "Arkansas Toothpicks." Editor: Bonnie Dixon Stanley, *The Heritage* 4, Hot Spring County, Arkansas, Historical Society, 1977: 14.

Thrasher, Thomas J. and compiled by *The Heritage* Committee/ed. staff of the Hot Spring County, Arkansas, Historical Society: Bonnie Jean Stanley, Lucile Mason, Ann Harp, Marcille Stiles, Martha Ann Henry, Ella Mae Cullins, Henry Erwin, Juanita Efird, and Bernice Roache. "Letters From a Confederate Soldier (Thomas J. Thrasher)" (Editors note the letters were contributed by Coleman C. Lowry from Jones Mills.) and "Chronology of Battle Engagements of the Hot Spring County Hornets (Rockport Volunteers)." *The Heritage* 15, Hot Spring County, Arkansas, Historical Society, 1988: 135-138 and 138-139.

MAGAZINES/NEWSPAPERS/JOURNALS

Beerstecher, Frances, ed. *Malvern Daily Record, 50th, 1916-1966, Fiftieth Anniversary Edition, 1916-1966, Vol. 51, no. 1,* Malvern, Arkansas: Malvern Daily Record, 1966.

Dickens, Charles. "Great Expectations, A Novel," *The Reissue of Harper's Weekly: A Journal of Civilization,* Listed by original *Harper's Weekly* publication information, 1860/1861: Original(s): Vol. 5, no. 210 (Saturday, January 5, 1861): Page number 5-6 ("Chapter 10"); Vol. 5, no. 211 (Saturday, January 12, 1861): *21-22* ("Chapter 11"); Vol. 5, no. 212 (Saturday, January 19, 1861): 46-47 ("Chapters 13-14"); Vol. 5, no. 214 (Saturday,

February 2, 1861): 69-70 ("Chapter 15 and 16")[Note: no chapters run in no. 213.]; Vol. 5, no. 215 (Saturday, February 9, 1861): 85-86 ("Chapter 17"); Vol. 5, no. 216 (Saturday, February 16, 1861): 101-102 ("Chapter 18"); Vol. 5, no. 217 (Saturday, February 23, 1861): 117-119 ("Chapter 19-20"); Vol. 5, no. 218 (Saturday, March 2, 1861): 133-134 ("Chapter 21"); Vol. 5, no. 219 (Saturday, March 9, 1861): 149-150 ("Chapter 22-23"); Vol. 5, no. 220 (Saturday, March 16, 1861): 173-175 ("Chapter 24-25"); Vol. 5, no. 221 (Saturday, March 23, 1861): 181-182 ("Chapter 26-27"); Vol. 5, no. 222, (Saturday, March 30, 1861): 205-206 ("Chapter 28"); Vol. 5, no. 223 (Saturday, April 6, 1861): 213-215 ("Chapter 29-30"); Vol. 5, no. 224 (Saturday, April 13, 1861): 229-230 ("Chapter 31-32"); Vol. 5, no. 225 (Saturday, April 20, 1861): 253-255 ("Chapter 33-34"); Vol. 5, no. 226, (Saturday, April 27, 1861): 269-271 ("Chapter 35-36"); Vol. 5, no. 227 (Saturday, May 4, 1861): 286-287 ("Chapter 37"); Vol. 5, no. 228 (Saturday, May 11, 1861): 301-302 ("Chapter 38"); Vol. 5, no. 229 (Saturday, May 18, 1861): 318-319 ("Chapter 39"); Vol.5, no. 230 (Saturday, May 25, 1861): 334-335 ("Chapter 40-41"). Original title of publication(s): *Harper's Weekly: A Journal of Civilization,* New York: Harper and Brothers, 1860, 1861. *Reissue(s)*: Vol. 1, no. 2-4, 6-22, weekly reissues from January 7-May 25, 1961, Living History Inc.: Shenandoah, Iowa: Living History, Inc., 1961.

Harper and Brothers publishers/eds.
"The Great Southern Movement" (Illustrations specified by the editors/publishers on front page and appearing throughout this issue.); "The Cotton Movement"18; "Domestic Intelligence" Section/column, 22-23: "Foreign News" section/column, 23, "England: A Hint to King Cotton."; "The Revolution at Charleston," 24-25 (Listed by original *Harper's Weekly* publication information, 1861). *The Reissue of Harper's Weekly: A Journal of Civilization,*Vol. 5, no. 211 (Saturday, January 12, 1861). Original title of publication: *Harper's Weekly: A Journal of Civilization,* New York: Harper and Brothers, 1860, 1861. *Reissue*: Vol. 1, no. 3, January 12, 1961, Living History Inc.: Shenandoah, Iowa: Living History, Inc., 1961.

Harper and Brothers publishers/eds.
"Domestic Intelligence" Section/column, 38-39; "Foreign News" Section, 39; "The First of the War," 40-42 (Listed by original *Harper's Weekly* publication information, 1861). *The Reissue of Harper's Weekly: A Journal of Civilization,* Vol. 5, no. 212, (Saturday, January 19, 1861). Original title of publication: *Harper's Weekly: A Journal of Civilization,* New York: Harper and Brothers, 1861. *Reissue*: Vol. 1, no. 4, January 19, 1961, Living History Inc.: Shenandoah, Iowa: Living History, Inc., 1961.

Harper and Brothers publishers/eds.
"The Prayer at Sumter"(Front page); "Fort Sumter" (starts on front page) 49-50; "Fort Moultrie at Present," 50; Note from publishers

on no issue of "Great Expectations" in this issue due to shipment delays, 50; "Domestic Intelligence" section/column, 54-55 (Listed by original *Harper's Weekly* publication information, 1861). *The Reissue of Harper's Weekly: A Journal of Civilization,*Vol. 5, no. 213 (Saturday, January 26, 1861). Original title of publication: *Harper's Weekly: A Journal of Civilization,* New York: Harper and Brothers, 1861. *Reissue*: Vol. 1, no. 5, January 26, 1961, Living History Inc.: Shenandoah, Iowa: Living History, Inc., 1961.

Harper and Brothers publishers/eds. "The Mississippi Delegation in Congress" Front page (65)-66; "High Treason" 66; "Domestic Intelligence" section/column, 70-71 (Listed by original *Harper's Weekly* publication information, 1861). The *Reissue of Harper's Weekly: A Journal of Civilization,*Vol. 5, no. 214 (Saturday, February 2, 1861). Original title of publication: *Harper's Weekly: A Journal of Civilization,* New York: Harper and Brothers,1861. *Reissue*: Vol. 1, no. 6, February 2, 1961, Living History Inc.: Shenandoah, Iowa: Living History, Inc., 1961.

Harper and Brothers publishers/eds. "The Seceding Alabama Delegation In Congress" Front Page (81)-82; "Domestic Intelligence" section/column, 86-87; "The Harbor of Pensacola," 89; "Montgomery, Alabama," 89; "Fort Monroe, Virginia," 89-90; "Vicksburg, Mississippi," 90 (Listed by original *Harper's Weekly* publication information,

1861). *The Reissue of Harper's Weekly: A Journal of Civilization,* Vol. 5, no. 215 (Saturday, February 9, 1861). Original title of publication: *Harper's Weekly: A Journal of Civilization,* New York: Harper and Brothers, 1861. *Reissue:* Vol. 1, no. 7, February 9, 1961, Living History Inc.: Shenandoah, Iowa: Living History, Inc., 1961.

Harper and Brothers publishers/eds. "Cotton Supply," 98; "Stay Laws," 98; "Fort Sumter," 100-101; "Domestic Intelligence" section/column,102-103 (Listed by original *Harper's Weekly* publication information, 1861). *The Reissue of Harper's Weekly: A Journal of Civilization,* Vol. 5, no. 216, (Saturday, February 16, 1861). Original title of publication: *Harper's Weekly: A Journal of Civilization,* New York: Harper and Brothers, 1861. *Reissue:* Vol. 1, no. 8, February 16, 1961, Living History Inc.: Shenandoah, Iowa: Living History, Inc., 1961.

Harper and Brothers publishers/eds. "The Sugar Question," 114; "Our Army and Navy," 114; "Domestic Intelligence" section/column, 119; "Foreign News" section/column: "England: British Views of Secession," 119; "Fort Pickens, Pensacola" sketch,120 and article, 122; "Fort Jefferson, Tortugas (Key West)," sketch, 121, and article, 122; "Map Showing the Comparative Area of the Northern and Southern States East of the Rocky Mountains. 1861," 124; "President Davis and Vice President Stephens" (sketches and article), 125 (Listed by original *Harper's Weekly* publication information, 1861). *The Reissue of Harper's Weekly: A Journal of Civilization,* Vol. 5, no. 217 (Saturday, February 23, 1861). Original title of publication: *Harper's Weekly: A Journal of Civilization,* New York: Harper and Brothers, 1861. *Reissue*: Vol. 1, no. 9, February 23, 1961, Living History Inc.: Shenandoah, Iowa: Living History, Inc., 1961.

Harper and Brothers publishers/eds. "European Opinion Upon Our Troubles," 130; "Patriotism," 130; "Domestic Intelligence" section/column, 134-135 (Listed by original *Harper's Weekly* publication information, 1861). *The Reissue of Harper's Weekly: A Journal of Civilization,* Vol. 5, no. 218 (Saturday, March 2, 1861). Original title of publication: *Harper's Weekly: A Journal of Civilization,* New York: Harper and Brothers, 1861. *Reissue*: Vol. 1, no. 10, March 2, 1961, Living History Inc.: Shenandoah, Iowa: Living History, Inc., 1961.

Harper and Brothers publishers/eds. "Reconstruction," 146; "Domestic Intelligence" section/column, 150-151: "Fort Smith and Little Rock Arsenal, Arkansas," 155-156; "President J. Davis's Inauguration at Montgomery," 156 (article)-157 (sketch) (Listed by original *Harper's Weekly* publication information, 1861). *The Reissue of Harper's Weekly: A Journal of Civilization,* Vol. 5, no. 219 (Saturday, March 9, 1861). Original title of publication: *Harper's Weekly, A Journal of*

Civilization, New York: Harper and Brothers, 1861. *Reissue*: Vol. 1, no. 11, March 9, 1961, Living History Inc.: Shenandoah, Iowa: Living History, Inc., 1961.

Harper and Brothers publishers/eds. "The Inauguration," 165-166 article and sketch, 168-169 sketch; "Domestic Intelligence" section/column,166-167; "The Forts In Texas," 172-173, sketches and article (Listed by original *Harper's Weekly* publication information, 1861). *The Reissue of Harper's Weekly: A Journal of Civilization,*Vol. 5, no. 220 (Saturday, March 16, 1861). Original title of publication: *Harper's Weekly: A Journal of Civilization,* New York: Harper and Brothers, 1861. *Reissue*: Vol. 1, no. 12, March 16, 1861, Living History Inc.: Shenandoah, Iowa: Living History, Inc., 1961.

Harper and Brothers publishers/eds. "General Twigg's Surrender to The Texans," 182 (article) and 184 (sketch); "Fort Lancaster," 182 (article) and 185 (sketch); "Fort Brown, Texas," 182-183; "Domestic Intelligence" section/column, 183 (Listed by original *Harper's Weekly* publication information, 1861). *The Reissue of Harper's Weekly: A Journal of Civilization,*Vol. 5, no. 221 (Saturday, March 23, 1861). Original title of publication: *Harper's Weekly: A Journal of Civilization,* New York: Harper and Brothers, 1861. *Reissue*: Vol. 1, no. 13, March 23, 1861, Living History Inc.: Shenandoah, Iowa: Living History, Inc., 1961.

Harper and Brothers publishers/eds. "The Two Constitutions," 194; "More Views of New Orleans," sketches and article, 196; "The Coast Line From Mississippi Mouth To Pensacola," map and article, 197;"Domestic Intelligence" section/column, 199; "General Sam Houston" article and sketch, 204 (Listed by original *Harper's Weekly* publication information, 1861). *The Reissue of Harper's Weekly: A Journal of Civilization,*Vol. 5, no. 222 (Saturday, March 30, 1861). Original title of publication: *Harper's Weekly: A Journal of Civilization,* New York: Harper and Brothers, 1861. *Reissue*: Vol. 1, no. 14, March 30, 1961, Living History Inc.: Shenandoah, Iowa: Living History, Inc., 1961.

Harper and Brothers publishers/eds. "Domestic Intelligence" section/column, 215; "Our Virginia Scenes" sketch, 216-217 and article, 218 (Listed by original *Harper's Weekly* publication information, 1861). *The Reissue of Harper's Weekly: A Journal of Civilization,*Vol.5, no. 223,Saturday, April 6, 1861. Original title of publication: *Harper's Weekly: A Journal of Civilization,* New York: Harper and Brothers, 1861. *Reissue*: Vol. 1, no. 15, April 6, 1961, Living History Inc.: Shenandoah, Iowa: Living History, Inc., 1961.

Harper and Brothers publishers/eds. "Domestic Intelligence" section/column, 231 (Listed by original *Harper's Weekly* publication information, 1861). *The Reissue of Harper's Weekly: A Journal of Civilization,*Vol. 5, no.

224 (Saturday, April 13, 1861). Original title of publication: *Harper's Weekly: A Journal of Civilization,* New York: Harper and Brothers, 1861. *Reissue*: Vol. 1, no. 16, April 13, 1961, Living History Inc.: Shenandoah, Iowa: Living History, Inc., 1961.

Harper and Brothers publishers/eds. "The Right of Secession," 242; "Domestic Intelligence," section/column, 247 (Listed by original *Harper's Weekly* publication information, 1861). *The Reissue of Harper's Weekly: A Journal of Civilization,* Vol. 5, no. 225, (Saturday, April 20, 1861). Original title of publication: *Harper's Weekly: A Journal of Civilization,* New York: Harper and Brothers, 1861. *Reissue*: Vol. 1, no. 17, April 20, 1961, Living History Inc.: Shenandoah, Iowa: Living History, Inc., 1961.

Harper and Brothers publishers/eds. "The Bombardment of Fort Sumter," Front page (257) article and sketches, 260-261, 265; "Swearing in Volunteers at Washington," Front page (257)-258, sketch and article; "A Proclamation," 258; "The War," 258; "Domestic Intelligence" section/column, 263 (Listed by original *Harper's Weekly* publication information, 1861). *The Reissue of Harper's Weekly: A Journal of Civilization,* Vol.5, no. 226 (Saturday, April 27, 1861).Original title of publication: *Harper's Weekly: A Journal of Civilization,* New York: Harper and Brothers, 1861. *Reissue*: Vol. 1, no. 18, April 27, 1961,

Living History Inc.: Shenandoah, Iowa: Living History, Inc., 1961.

Harper and Brothers publishers/eds. "The War," 274; "The Lounger" section/column, 274; "Domestic Intelligence" section/column, 275; "Our War Illustrations," article 279; Map, 276; Sketches, 277, 280-285 (Listed by original *Harper's Weekly* publication information, 1861). *The Reissue of Harper's Weekly: A Journal of Civilization,* Vol. 5, no. 227 *(*Saturday, May 4, 1861). Original title of publication: *Harper's Weekly: A Journal of Civilization,* New York: Harper and Brothers, 1861. *Reissue*: Vol 1, no. 19, May 4, 1961, Living History Inc.: Shenandoah, Iowa: Living History, Inc., 1961.

Harper and Brothers publishers/eds. "A Few Figures," 290; "The Lounger" section/column, 290; "Domestic Intelligence" section/column, 291; "Our War Illustrations," 291-293, article and sketches; "Our War Pictures," 294-301, article and sketches (Listed by original *Harper's Weekly* publication information, 1861). *The Reissue of Harper's Weekly: A Journal of Civilization,* Vol. 5, no. 228 *(*Saturday, May 11, 1861). Original title of publication: *Harper's Weekly: A Journal of Civilization,* New York: Harper and Brothers, 1861. *Reissue*: Vol. 1, no. 20, May 11, 1961, Living History Inc.: Shenandoah, Iowa: Living History, Inc., 1961.

Harper and Brothers publishers/eds. "Mr. Jefferson Davis's 'Message'" 306; "The

Lounger" section/column, 306-307; "Domestic Intelligence" section/column, 307; war sketches, Front page(305), 308-318 (Listed by original *Harper's Weekly* publication information, 1861). *The Reissue of Harper's Weekly: A Journal of Civilization,*Vol. 5, no. 229 *(*Saturday, May 18, 1861). Original title of publication: *Harper's Weekly: A Journal of Civilization,* New York: Harper and Brothers, 1861. *Reissue*: Vol 1, no. 21, May 18, 1961, Living History Inc.: Shenandoah, Iowa: Living History, Inc., 1961.

Harper and Brothers publishers/eds. "To Our Southern Readers," 322; "Domestic Intelligence" section/column, 323 (Listed by original *Harper's Weekly* publication information, 1861). *The Reissue of Harper's Weekly: A Journal of Civilization,* Vol. 5, no. 230 (Saturday, May 25, 1861) Original title of publication: *Harper's Weekly: A Journal of Civilization,* New York: Harper and Brothers, 1861. *Reissue*: Vol. 1, no. 22, May 25, 1961, Living History Inc.: Shenandoah, Iowa: Living History, Inc., 1961.

WEBSITES-ONLINE WORKS

Alexander, Kathy/Legends of America, comp. and ed. "Fort Delaware, Delaware City, Delaware." Updated January 2023. *Legends of America* website. Accessed 10/16/2023. https://www.legendsofamerica.com/fort-delaware-delaware-city/

American Battlefield Trust. "10 Facts: The Battle of Chickamauga: September 18-20,

1863." Accessed 9/28/2023. https://www.battlefields.org/learn/articles/10-facts-battle-chickamauga.

Arkansas: AR GenWeb Project and The US GenWeb Project. "Welcome to Benton County Arkansas: Arkansas Confederate Regimental Histories: Infantry." Section: "Third Arkansas Infantry Regiment." Accessed 6/7/2023. http://argenweb.net/benton/military/cw-confed-inf.html#2ndBatn.

Betts, Vicki, "[Little Rock] Arkansas True Democrat, 1860." (2016). By Title. Paper 75. Accessed 9/26/2023. http://hdl.handle.net/10950/711.

Britannica, T. Editors of Encyclopaedia. "Battle of Antietam." *Encyclopedia Britannica.* (Site completes periodic updates) Accessed 9/10/2023. https://www.britannica.com/event/Battle-of-Antietam.

Christ, Mark K., Arkansas Historic Preservation Program. "Little Rock Campaign, AKA: Arkansas Expedition." *CALS (Central Arkansas Library System), Encyclopedia of Arkansas*. Date of last update: June 16, 2023 as of date accessed. Accessed 9/28/2023. https://encyclopediaofarkansas.net/entries/little-rock-campaign-517/.

Coffey, Walter. "The Cheat Mountain Expedition." Date of article: September 15, 2021 on *The Civil War Months* website. Accessed 9/16/2023.

https://civilwarmonths.com/2021/09/15/the-cheat-mountain-expedition/.

Cometti, Elizabeth, ed. *West Virginia History (A copyright publication of West Virginia Archives and History).* "Excerpts from "Prison Life at Fort Delaware."" vol. 2, no. 2 (January 1941), 120-141 and no. 3 (April 1941), 217-230. Accessed 10/16/2023. https://archive.wvculture.org/history/journal_wvh/wvh2-1.html.

Dingess, Rebecca and Clio Admin. "The Battle of Bayou Fourche." *Clio: Your Guide to History.* (November 18, 2015). Accessed 10/18/2023. https://theclio.com/entry/9019.

Dougan, Michael B. (Jonesboro, Arkansas). "Elementary and Secondary Education." *CALS Encyclopedia of Arkansas.* July 1, 2023: Last date updated as of date accessed. Accessed 10/15/2023. https://encyclopediaofarkansas.net/entries/elementary-and-secondary-education-389/.

Elmore, Tom. "Repulse of Robertson's Brigade in the Rose Woods in the Opening Attack on July 2." *Civil War Talk* website (May 13, 2021). Accessed 9/1/2023. https://civilwartalk.com/threads/repulse-of-robertson's-brigade-in-the-rose-woods-in-the-opening-attack-on-july-2.185103/.

Gettysburg Greg. "Manning's Ledge in Rose Woods." *Civil War Talk website* (May 23, 2023). Accessed 9/1/2023. https://civilwartalk.com/threads/mannings-ledge-in-rose-woods.202613/.

Gettysburg National Military Park and Rosiecki, Casimer (Park Ranger). "Gettysburg in My Hometown: Lieut. Col. Taylor, 20th Indiana Infantry." (Sept. 18, 2014) Blog post featured on *From The Fields of Gettysburg: The Blog of Gettysburg National Military Park.* Accessed 9/3/2023. https://npsgnmp.wordpress.com/2014/09/18/gettysburg-in-my-hometown-lieut-col-taylor-20th-indiana-infantry/.

Gregory, R.W., comp. "Nineteenth Century Guard Duty." *Regimental Dispatch.* (Oct., Dec. 1999 and Jan., 2000). Accessed 9/20/2023. https://www.21vafco.org/19thCenturyGuardDuty.html.

Gresham, John D. "Civil War Artillery." *Warfare History Network.* Accessed 10/12/2023. https://warfarehistorynetwork.com/civil-war-artillery/.

Hamacher, Dave. "Licensed Battlefield Guide Dave Hamacher: Texas Brigade Part 2." *Gettysburg Daily.* (April 2, 2012). Accessed 10/23/2023. https://www.gettysburgdaily.com/licensed-battlefield-guide-dave-hamacher-texas-brigade-part-2/.

Hamacher, Dave. "Licensed Battlefield Guide Dave Hamacher: Texas Brigade Part 3." *Gettysburg Daily.* (April 9, 2012). Accessed 10/23/2023. https://www.gettysburgdaily.com/licensed-battlefield-guide-dave-hamacher-texas-brigade-part-3/.

Hardy, Michael C. "Hardtack v. Flour v. Cornmeal." May 20, 2020, featured on blog "Looking for the Confederate War: Historian Michael C. Hardy's quest to understand Confederate history, from the boots up." Accessed 10/7/2023. http://michaelchardy.blogspot.com/2020/05/hardtack-v-flour-v-corn-meal.html.

Hawks, Steve A, *The Civil War in the East* website. "3rd Arkansas Infantry Regiment: *Confederate Infantries and Batteries* Arkansas."* Accessed 6/7/2023. https://civilwarintheeast.com/confederate-regiments/arkansas/3rd-arkansas/

Lansingburgh Historical Society. *Lansingburgh Historical Society* website. "Sweet Potato Coffee (1861)" (November 27, 2017). Accessed 10/3/2023. https://www.lansingburghhistoricalsociety.org/in-the-news/sweet-potato-coffee-1861.

Latschar, Terry. "My brave Texans, forward and take those heights." *Jerome Bonaparte Robertson and The Texas Brigade.* (Featured on NPS history website.) Accessed 8/31/2023. http://npshistory.com/series/symposia/gettysburg_seminars/9/essay6.pdf.

Marvel, William. "A Poor Man's Fight." *National Park Civil War Series, The Civil War's Common Soldier.* Accessed 9/11/2023.

https://www.nps.gov/parkhistory/online_books/c ivil_war_series/3/sec2.htm.

Montgomery, Robin. "Opinion: Hood's Famous Texas Brigade: The Trans-Brazos Connection" (Dec. 6, 2022). Accessed 6/10/2023. https://www.itemonline.com/opinion/opinion-hood-s-famous-texas-brigade-the-trans-brazos-connection/article_83a8ff78-7574-11ed-b9e6-ff96a920f74e.html.

Myers, Mark L., Sergeant Major, USA. "The Role of the NCO During the Civil War" (April 5, 2004). Accessed 9/20/2023. *https://acrobat.adobe.com/id/urn:aaid:sc:US:f4 939e76-b334-426b-acdb-df551535fad9*.

National Park Service, U.S. Department of the Interior. *National Park Service* website. Ulysses S. Grant Historic Site, Article: "Air Balloons in the Civil War." Accessed 9/26/2023. https://www.nps.gov/articles/000/air-balloons-in-the-civil-war.htm.

Owen, Joe. ECW Guest Post, *Emerging Civil War* website. Posted October 15, 2021. "The Texas Color Bearer at Devil's Den." Accessed 9/27/2023. https://emergingcivilwar.com/2021/10/15/the-texas-color-bearer-at-devils-den/.

Pennel, Emily, Education Outreach Coordinator for the Arkansas Historic Preservation Program (Little Rock, Ark.) (An Agency of the Department of Arkansas Heritage); Rewritten and Redesigned by Shelle Stormoe, 2016. "Hallowed Ground: Arkansas's Historic Places in the Civil War: Learning from

Statewide Historic Places." Accessed 9/28/2023. https://www.arkansasheritage.com/docs/default-source/ahpp-documents/teaching-materials/hallowedgroundlessonplan2016.pdf?sfvrsn=a2762507_2.

Rhodes, Sonny. University of Arkansas at Little Rock. "Newspapers During the Civil War." CALS (Central Arkansas Library System), Encyclopedia of Arkansas, last updated September 1, 2022. Accessed 9/28/2023. https://encyclopediaofarkansas.net/entries/newspapers-during-the-civil-war-7896/.

Robertson, William G. (Text), Maps by George Skoch. Information from the *National Park Civil War Series, The Battle of Chickamauga*, Published by Eastern National, copyright 1995. (Information listed on Cover Page section of the website.) Portion from the History E-Library website accessed. "Civil War Series: The Battle for Chickamauga." (*Note: corrected spelling of "battes" to "battle".) "Noon to Mid Afternoon, Saturday, September 1863." Accessed 10/3/23 https://www.nps.gov/parkhistory/online_books/civil_war_series/10/sec5.htm.

Roy, Benjamin M. "Close, But No Cigar: Tobacco Usage During the Civil War Era."(2020). *Student Publications*. 886. https://cupola.gettysburg.edu/student_scholarship/886. Accessed on 10/9/23 from The Cupola: Scholarship at Gettysburg College website. https://cupola.gettysburg.edu/cgi/viewcontent.cgi?article=1964&context=student_scholarship.

Smith, Mrs. Mary Grimes; Rodman, Lida T.; Hoyt, E. M. B., McDonald, Mrs. John; Grimes, Mrs. J. Bryan, eds. *The Confederate Reveille: Memorial Edition.* The Pamlico Chapter of the Daughters of the Confederacy, Washington, N. C., May 10, 1898, Raleigh: Edwards and Broughton, Printers and Binders, 1898. Accessed 10/7/2023. https://tile.loc.gov/storage-services/public/gdcmassbookdig/confederaterevei00unit/confederaterevei00unit.pdf.

Stailey, James Sr. January 5, 2007 forum on genealogy.com website, "3rd Arkansas Infantry @ Gettysburg . . . John Allen Wilkerson." From a story written by Mauriel P. Joslyn, *Gettysburg Magazine.* Accessed 9/1/2023. https://www.genealogy.com/forum/general/topics/civilwar/22854/.

Steelhammer, Rick. Posted on *West Virginia Land and Trust* website on February 14, [?]. "Camp Bartow: A Civil War Site Protected: West Virginia Land Trust preserves site of Civil War battle, camp." *Charleston Gazette.* Accessed 11/7/2023. https://www.wvlandtrust.org/news-items/1583/.

Swain, Craig (Leesburg, Virginia) (text and photos). Submitted August 8, 2010, page revised June 16, 2016 on the *HMdb.org: The Historical Marker Database.* "Camp Bartow, Battle of Greenbrier River, The First

Campaign." Accessed 11/7/2023. *https://www.hmdb.org/m.asp?m=34168*.

The Gettysburg Diographics website, "The Gettysburg Diographs: Fine Art Prints of the Battle of Gettysburg" page and "Scenes of Houck's Ridge" section. Accessed 9/1/2023. https://diographics.com/houcks-ridge.

Zeller, Bob. "How Photos From the Battle of Antietam Revealed the American Civil War's Horrors." September 14, 2021, updated August 4, 2023. *History.com.* Accessed 9/20/2023. https://www.history.com/news/battle-antietam-photography-civil-war.

EDUCATIONAL VIDEOS

Videos from *American Battlefield Trust* via their YouTube channel also provided historical insight of the battlefields. Viewed during 2023.